BAD REPUTATION

JESSA JAMES

Bad Reputation: Copyright © 2020 by Jessa James

All Rights Reserved. No part of this book may be reproduced or transmitted in any form or by any means, electrical, digital or mechanical including but not limited to photocopying, recording, scanning or by any type of data storage and retrieval system without express, written permission from the author.

Published by Jessa James
James, Jessa
Bad Reputation

Cover design copyright 2020 by Jessa James, Author
Images/Photo Credit: Design Credit: BookCoverForYou

Publisher's Note:
This book was written for an adult audience. The book may contain explicit sexual content. Sexual activities included in this book are strictly fantasies intended for adults and any activities or risks taken by fictional characters within the story are neither endorsed nor encouraged by the author or publisher.

This book has been previously published.

GET A FREE BOOK!

Join my mailing list to be the first to know of new releases, free books, special prices and other author giveaways.

http://freehotcontemporary.com

1

EMMA

Jameson

We fuck until dawn. Jameson seems unusually demanding and possessive, driving both of us to the very edge of sanity. And I am so happy to be with him, to kiss him and hold him... even to be brutalized and punished by him...

I love it. I can't get enough of Jameson, it seems.

Afterwards, exhausted and sleep deprived, I fall asleep in Jameson's arms. I sleep fitfully, tossing and turning. Even in sleep, I know something is wrong. I just can't figure out for the life of me what it is.

As the first fingers of morning creep into through the window, I slip out of bed. Padding down the hall to the bathroom, I sit down and pee. I look over at the little pink plastic chest of drawers that Evie insisted upon when we first moved in.

"It's to keep our necessities in," she said. She dropped her voice to a whisper. "You know, our *lady time* necessities."

I smile at that. She apparently thinks that we need to hide our tampons and pads, in our own bathroom. I get up, going to wash my hands. I turn on the water, run my hands underneath, and then stop.

Turning a little to look over my shoulder, I eye the chest of drawers. It's been a while since I have needed to use anything from inside the chest. How long has it been?

I turn off the tap, wiping my hands on a towel. Doing some math in my head, I realize that it's been… almost seven weeks since my last period. And I've been sleeping with Jameson for… almost a month…

"Shit." I glance at myself in the mirror. "There's no way that… you're definitely not…"

I do the math again, then bite my lip. It could be the stress from finals. Or it could be some kind of secret stress from the pressure not to let Asher know about my relationship with his best friend. That could play a role, definitely.

It could also be nothing.

I open the drawers, digging around, hoping to find a pregnancy test. Of course there are none; both of the women in this house are on birth control, as far as I know.

I bite my lip. I'm probably freaking out over nothing.

Still… I will feel so much better if I take a test, just to be sure. Slipping out of the bathroom, I decide to get to the pharmacy as soon as possible. Better to just put a thought like that to bed, right away.

Once I reach the bedroom though, I know that something is up with Jameson. He's sitting on the side of the bed, totally dressed, his head hanging low. When he looks at me, his expression is tormented.

I close the door behind myself. "Jameson, what's wrong?"

He takes a breath. "I don't want to see you any more, Emma. Or… I don't know. I can't."

My brows shoot up. "What? What are you talking about?"

He stands up, pacing a little in the narrow space beside the bed.

"I talked to Asher yesterday."

I'm taken aback. "I thought he wasn't talking to you still."

"Well, he changed his mind."

I put my hands on my hips. "That's nice, but it has nothing to do with *us*."

Jameson looks at me, his eyes dark. "It was never supposed to turn into this... this... whatever it is, that's between us. It wasn't even supposed to happen at all."

I glare at him. "And yet, it did. Here you are, in my bedroom."

He runs his hands over his face for a second, clearly frustrated.

"I shouldn't have let it happen."

"But you did."

"And I'm trying to undo it!" he shouts. "I'm trying to save us, Emma. Jesus fucking christ, can't you see that?"

"I'm sorry, did you say you were trying to *save* us?" I snarl. "As in, you are trying to save us both? Save us from what?"

"Emma..." he says, clenching his jaw. "We have nothing in common. We're not even remotely connected, except through my *best friend*. And yesterday he reminded me—"

"Reminded you??!"

"Yes! He reminded me of the fact that he's been there for me when nobody else even gave a damn if I lived or died! He helped me when there was no one else. I... I *owe* him, big time."

"That doesn't mean that you owe him your life!" I snap, growing frazzled. "When will you have paid your debt, Jameson? Huh? Five more years? Ten more? Tell me, what is the plan, exactly?"

I see a flash of pain in his eyes. "There is almost nothing I wouldn't give up if he asked me to."

"I'm one of those things, then? You can just... just decide to stop being in a relationship—"

"We were never in a relationship!!" he hisses. "At best, we had a fling. And now, it's *over*."

My eyes fill with tears. He means it. This isn't just another *we really shouldn't* moment.

"You want out?" I say, controlling my voice to keep from screaming at him. "There's the door. No one is stopping you."

His expression hardens. "It's better this way."

"Fuck you," I whisper, looking away as tears start to spill down my cheeks, hot and wet. I wipe them away with the back of my hand. "I mean it. Go straight to hell, Jameson Hart."

He hesitates for a few moments, then shakes his head. "It's better if I do it this way than—"

"Get. *Out!*" I scream at him. "No more explaining! Just go!"

He rips the door of my room open, the expression on his face grimmer than any I've ever seen.

And I'm left in my bedroom, alone, sobbing over him.

What am I going to do?

2

EMMA

I curl into a ball on my bed, among the messy sheets, and bawl like a baby. Not pretty crying, although I'm not sure there is even such a thing. No, I cry ugly tears, my face red and puffy, with snot running everywhere. I'm not quiet about it either. I sob into one of my pillows and make great big gasping sounds.

I'm feeling bereft. I keep replaying what Jameson said to me, standing here in the doorway.

"We were never in a relationship!! At best, we had a fling. And now, it's over."

That hurts more than anything else he could have said. Because he's right about one thing... we never defined the thing between us, never gave it a name. Clearly what I thought was so amazing and earth shattering, Jameson thought was nothing more than a *fling*.

Maybe Asher is right. Maybe Jameson really is bad news, running through women like a hot knife through butter.

It definitely didn't feel that way when I looked into Jameson's eyes, but... I'm starting to question every single moment we were together, every impulse and thought that I had.

I think about Asher again, about his stupid rule and his weird hold on Jameson. Obviously I have missed something in their history together, because Jameson is so devoted to Asher... and Asher seems not to notice.

My tears dry up, until I remember that my period is late. Somehow, in all the breaking up madness, I've managed to completely dismiss the most important fact of all.

I could be pregnant with Jameson's child.

The potential ramifications of that fact echo through my brain. I can't even begin to cope with that. The uncertainty is killing me.

So I drag myself out of bed, putting on a pair of dark yoga pants and a billowy tee shirt that says GUCCI. I am sure that my face still looks puffy, and my outfit is thrown together from the bottom of my closet...

But at least I'm not crying right now, in this moment. After slipping on a pair of dark blue Converse, I open the door to my bedroom.

I surprise Evie, who is in front of my bedroom door, about to knock. She's dressed in a pair of jeans and a baggy Hilary 2016 hoodie.

"Hey..." she says, her brown eyes wide. "I thought I heard you crying. You seem... maybe not okay?"

I glance down at myself, and my chin starts to wobble again. My eyes well up instantly, and I shake my head.

"I got dumped... and I might be pregnant," I say, my words tremulous as my face collapses in tears.

"Whoa, whoa," Evie says, her brow furrowing. She pulls me into her arms, hugging me tightly. "That's... a lot. Here, come with me into the kitchen."

I let Evie guide me down the hallway, into the tiny kitchen. She sits me down in one of the chairs at the table, and hands me a clean dish towel. I wipe at my face with it, feeling stupid.

"I'll make us some herbal tea," she says. "And you can start telling me what happened."

She goes to fill the kettle up. I am sitting in one of our hard-backed kitchen chairs, trying to control my crying. Evie doesn't press me further. She just reaches in the cupboards for two mugs and the box of tea bags, going about it as though I wasn't even present.

For some reason, that calms me down a little. I close my eyes and focus on my breathing for a few minutes. The kettle whistles, the noise brash and loud. When I open my eyes again, Evie is pouring boiling water into two mugs.

"Here, it's a citrus chamomile blend," Evie says, depositing a mug before me. "It's really comforting, I think. I've been going through sachet after sachet the last few weeks."

I curl my hands around the mug, feeling the warmth of its contents. I peer inside, and see a yellowish curl blossoming at the bottom of the cup. I squint. I'm trying to piece together something that Evie has just said, about using a lot of sachets and comfort…

"So… you want to tell me more about the breakup? Or would you rather start with the pregnancy?" Evie says, cool as a cucumber. She looks off into the distance for a moment. "Wait, let's just start with the breakup first."

I blink at her, but she just blows on her mug of tea. "Umm… okay…"

She studies me, her eyes warm. "I'm guessing that it was with Jameson?"

I wipe a tear from the corner of one eye, nodding. "Yeah."

"That figures. He's a rat bastard, for what it's worth."

That draws a strange noise from me, something like a mix between a chuckle and a grunt.

Evie takes a moment to dunk her tea bag a few times, then takes a sip. "Mmm. Alright, so. How long have you guys been hooking up?"

I clear my throat, twisting the tea bag's string around. "About two months. Maybe a little more."

"And was it serious? I mean, of course it was serious, because look at you. But like... did you guys... use boyfriend and girlfriend, or like... say I love you?"

I shake my head, unable to look up from the table. "No."

She wrinkles up her face, thinking. "But you felt deeply, I am guessing."

"Yeah. I mean, I definitely felt like..." I pause, gathering my thoughts. "I felt like I'd found that one person who just... gets it. Or gets me? I don't know. Maybe everyone that you have sex with is supposed to be like that, but—"

"Wait, you gave him your virginity?" Evie asks. Her brows shoot up. "Damn, girl."

I take a minute with that, sipping my tea. It is sort of comforting, the citrus flavor and herbal scent.

"I've been in love with Jameson for years," I finally admit. It's kind of a relief, saying it out loud to someone. "Like, ever since I was old enough to have dirty dreams. I kind of always thought, in the back of my head, that we would get together. I planned to give him my v-card since I was fifteen, before I even knew what that really entailed."

Evie's eyes go so wide, it's almost comical. "Wait, you were like... *saving yourself* for Jameson?"

I shrug, blushing. "Yeah, I was. I mean, it wasn't intentional for the last couple of years. But when I started to get *'I'm attracted to you'* signals off of him, I sort of... I really, really wanted to make it happen."

"Girlllllll," she says, excited. "I can't believe you've had a thing for him for so long! And I can't believe I didn't know about it."

I bite my lip and shrug a shoulder. "Doesn't matter, because of Asher."

She sits up a little straighter. "Asher? What does he have to do with anything?"

"Asher made up this stupid rule ages ago. He told Jameson and Forest and Gunnar not to sleep with me. Actually, he's told Gunnar several times to back off, because Gunnar is..." I search for the right word.

"A slut?" Evie's mouth curls upward.

"Yeah. Anyway, that rule has existed since I got boobs, I think. Because clearly I can't make my own decisions about who I sleep with. If it wasn't for the rule, I would just fall into bed with every guy I see!" I say sarcastically. "Meanwhile, Asher has no rules about who he can sleep with or date."

Evie looks down at the table, tracing something absentmindedly. "That doesn't sound fair."

"Thank you! It isn't." I sit back, trying to reach for my righteous indignation, but it's not there. I'm too busy being sad for any other emotions to register.

"So… are you ready to talk about the other thing yet?" she says gently.

My heart starts hammering just thinking about it. I give her a slow nod. "Yeah, I think so. I just… I'm on an IUD."

She cocks her head. "And yet you think you might be pregnant?"

My eyes fill with tears again. I feel pathetic. "Yes."

Evie considers me for a minute. "I'm assuming that you don't have happy feelings about that."

I take a sip of my tea, to keep myself calm. Then I take a breath. "I mean, I am very conflicted about it. On one hand, the fifteen year old version of myself is like… squealing with excitement. I've loved this guy for half my life, and now I'm going to have his baby? Like… I couldn't have imagined a better outcome, in the most selfish way."

She purses her lips. "And on the other hand?"

"Well, the downsides are twofold. First, I doubt that fifteen year old girl would be particularly happy that Jameson dumped me. And second, I'm in frigging law school! During the year, I study and go to school, from the time I wake up to the time I go to sleep. That's it. I don't have time for anything else. Adding a baby to that is like… a recipe for disaster."

"Definitely. I mean, you could handle it, but you wouldn't want to."

"Exactly. But... there is still a part of me that is like, going baby crazy. I'm imagining how amazing our child would be. Like have you ever seen baby shoes? Because they are so freaking cute. And I can see us when she's a little older. Me, dressing her up for her first ballet recital..."

I let the conversation lapse for a minute, daydreaming of pink hair bows. In my mind, Jameson is also there, because I think if he knew I was pregnant, he would insist on marrying me.

I squint, speculative. Is that crazy? I'm pretty sure that is crazy.

She clears her throat. "I mean, that does sound terribly nice."

I shake my head. "I think that I'm massively oversimplifying a very complex situation. If I were to be pregnant, and I were to decide to keep it, things between Jameson and I would be... well, complex is a nice way of saying it."

"Wellllll..." she says. "You don't even know if you have to worry about it. And there's a pretty easy way to figure out whether you do. So... you know, first things first."

I sigh. "We don't even have any pregnancy tests here. I checked."

She stands up. "We totally do. I know where they are. Now make sure you drink the rest of that tea, it's a little bit of a diuretic."

I narrow my eyes at her, but she's already flouncing out of the room. I down the rest of the mug of quickly cooling tea, then head into the hallway. She meets me, coming out of her room.

"Here," she says, handing me the plastic wrapped testing stick. "You pee on the end, then wait two minutes. Then we'll know what we're dealing with."

I take the test from her, my brow furrowing. "How does it work? I mean, how do we know if it's right?"

"Those things are like 95% accurate. Just pee on the end, and then we'll see what we have to be worried about."

Taking a deep breath, I head to the bathroom. I make quick

work out of peeing on the stick, then set the test on the counter and open the bathroom door. Evie is leaning against the wall when I open it.

"Done?" she asks.

"Yeah, just waiting now." I glance at the test, ready for it to be done.

But in my heart, I can't decide what I want the results to be.

If it's positive, my life as I know it is over. There's no questioning that. I'll have to drop out of law school. I'll have to deal with the looks of disappointment and anger on my family's faces. Worse, I'll have to tell Jameson.

On the other hand, though, I would be remiss if I didn't say that I am a little excited. A baby is a big change and a lot of responsibility, but it would Jameson's baby. I'd have a little piece of him, come what may.

"Emma, I think you can check now," Evie says gently.

I glance at her, as nervous I've ever been. With trembling hands, I reach for the test. I take a huge breath, then look.

It's negative. I look at Evie, feeling tears of relief form in my eyes.

"Negative," I say, bracing myself on the sink. I close my eyes. "Oh god. Thank the lord."

"That's good," Evie says, hugging me from behind. "Now your life doesn't have to change at all."

I put the test down and turn around to give her a real hug. I bury my face in her black hair, taking a long breath. "Thank you for holding my hand through this."

"Of course," she says simply. "It's what girls do for one another."

I pull back. "You know what else they do? Call for a breakup pizza."

She laughs. "It's pretty early in the day for that. How do you feel about me whipping us up some breakup omelets instead?"

I smile at her. "Okay. It's a deal. But I demand that we have pizza and ice cream delivered by the end of the day. I'm feeling like eating my emotions today."

"Deal."

Evie pushes off the wall, and I throw the test in the bathroom trash. I'm a little sad still, and I'm sure that it will come and go in waves…

But at least I'm not pregnant. Things could always be worse.

3
JAMESON

One Month Later
I slam on the brakes of my Jeep in the parking lot of the grocery store, gritting my teeth at the person who is backing out of the space in front of me. The car is an old Buick, and the driver is no doubt ancient, but I'm still irritated.

If I'm honest, everything is irritating these days. I had Asher to hang out with and complain about life to for about a week after my break up with Emma. But then he disappeared, and has yet to reappear.

I haven't seen or heard from Emma either, not that I can really blame her. It wasn't the smoothest break up ever, for either of us.

I maneuver my car into a spot, getting out. We ran out of all the citrus fruits at Cure, so here I am, finding a shopping cart. I wheel a cart inside, and veer to the right into the produce section.

The produce here is good and cheap. There's tons of greenery and colorful vegetables, all lined up in those black coolers that mist every once in a while. I turn to the stacks of citrus crates and grab handfuls of lemons, limes, oranges, and grapefruits.

Then I reconsider, and just grab one crate of each kind of citrus, stacking them in my shopping cart. I scowl down at the produce. I have a handful of other things to get while I'm at the grocery store, so I push my cart onward.

I can't stop thinking of Emma. I think about her here. I think about her at the movies. I think of her driving down the highway, and when I'm at the beach.

I know that I should forget all about her. After all, I pretty much told her that we weren't ever a thing. But somehow, I can't.

Instead, I replay for about the thousandth time the bits of information I've gotten about her from our mutual friends. I asked Evie how Emma was doing about two weeks ago. I got a stony stare in return. Evie raised a brow, and told me that Emma is just fine.

Her chilly attitude let me know that Emma told her everything... and that Evie didn't approve of how I handled the situation. I didn't need any of Evie's disapproval. I have plenty of my own misgivings without her adding salt to the wound.

I push my cart down the cereal aisle and grab my favorite brand of granola. I broke down and asked Asher about his sister last week, when we were working together. He just gave me a weird look and said that she's fine.

So that's all I know. She's fine. She's just... gone.

From my life, anyway. I would've expected to see her in Cure maybe, or hanging out with Asher at some point. After all, she has always just sort of shown up before this.

Now, I guess I ruined that.

I wander down the aisles, a faint squeaking coming from my cart. It's been a month, and I'm just feeling stuck.

Stuck in life. Stuck on her. I've never been in a relationship whose half-life was so long. Hell, I've never mourned a fling for more than a few days.

And that's what I told her we had. Just a fling.

The hurt on her face when I said that... it will haunt me forever. That was the moment that I would take back if I could.

But then of course, nothing would have been fixed or resolved. I would've been on a collision course with Asher, for sure.

I turn the cart around the end of an aisle, heading back to the front. At the far end of the aisle, looking at different types of pasta, is Emma.

I freeze, staring at her. She looks as beautiful as I remember, with her long raven locks tucked up in a crown braid. Her svelte figure is neatly wrapped in a sundress, and she's wearing those insanely tall heels that show off her legs.

I swear, if I was a cartoon, I would be a wolf, with my tongue rolling out and my eyes shaped like hearts. She senses someone looking at her and glances my way.

After getting used to her sunny smile and warm greeting whenever she saw me, I'm blown away by her black look. She scowls at me, turning to push her cart away as fast as she can go. She disappears around the corner.

Abandoning my cart where I was standing, I all but sprint in her direction. It takes a second for me to find her, a few aisles down, but I take advantage of my height and speed.

"Emma," I call to her, halfway down the aisle.

The look she throws over her shoulder is pure ice. I pay no heed, just hurry up. By the end of the aisle, I've caught up with her.

"Emma, please wait."

She stops, hesitation in every movement, and then turns around. She doesn't look very happy to see me. "What?"

"I just... I wanted to see you. You know, make sure you're doing okay," I say lamely.

She rubs one of her temples. "I'm okay. You've seen me."

She starts to turn away again, and I reach out and grab her arm. She looks at my hand like it is the devil, trying to gain access to her soul. She wrenches herself away.

"What are you trying to do here, exactly?" she hisses.

"Sorry," I say, stepping back and holding my hands up. "I just... I don't know. I've been trying to check up on you for a while."

She looks pissed. "Here I am. You've seen me. Are you happy with that?"

"No," I admit honestly. "I was hoping that we could... you know, still hang out. Be friends, go to restaurants."

She squints at me. "You mean you want things to go back to the way they were before we had sex?"

"Yeah. I was thinking we could—"

She tosses her head. "You realize that's friendzoning, right? Like, hey you, I want you to do all the things with me that I should do with a romantic parter, but without the romance."

"I mean, just because we broke up—"

"I didn't think flings got breakups."

Yeah, I deserved that one. "I think we can be friends still."

"Really? I don't."

We just stand there for a second, looking at each other. Fuck, I didn't expect negotiating things to be this hard with her. I have to come up with something to stop the hatred, and fast.

"I need your help," comes out of my mouth, without me even really thinking about it.

Emma raises an eyebrow. "Oh?"

"Yep. Uh... with studying for the GED. Yeah, I'm hopeless at studying by myself. I already had to put off my tests again for another month." It's true that I delayed my testing, but it isn't because I can't study alone. I just haven't been in the mood lately, at all.

"I don't know..." she says, her brow furrowing.

I go for the gusto. "It's just, I feel so stupid when I try to study by myself. Like, I know that I should be able to, but..."

I try to look pathetic. If you've ever been my height and tried to make a face like a pouty little kid, you know what I'm talking about.

She looks at me, and I can see her wavering. She's mad as hell still, but apparently my education is more important than that. She chews her lower lip.

I know what she needs to hear. She thinks I am pathetic, that I can't study by myself. I swallow the lump of pride that collects in my throat. I say the magic words, lowering my voice.

"Please? I can't do it on my own. I need help."

Emma's eyes narrow. For a second, I think she's about to yell at me. But she doesn't. Instead, she sighs and looks really annoyed with herself.

"Fine," she bites off, crossing her arms.

I feel my cheek heat; I'm ashamed of myself. Not only for having to take the damn GED in the first place, but for using it as an excuse to get Emma to forgive me.

"Thank you," I say, laying my hand on her arm.

She pulls away, like I am made of hot coals. Her face scrunches up. She looks actually wounded, like me touching her arm is an unforgivable sin. "Don't touch me."

My face heats a little more. "Sorry."

I see her own cheeks start to flush. "We need... we need boundaries."

I raise an eyebrow. "Boundaries? Like what?"

She rubs her arm where I touched her, looking angry. "Like no touching, for a start. And no... like, brooding."

"No brooding." I honesty try to keep a straight face, but I can't quite manage it.

My lips lift a little, and her mood suddenly darkens. The look in her green eyes is almost violent. She glares at me.

"If you're not going to take me seriously, you can study by yourself."

"No no," I say, raising my hands. "You make the rules, okay?"

"Damn right, I do." She looks hostile towards me.

"So, uh..." I rub the back of my neck. "Should I come over tomorrow night, then?"

"What? Uh, no. We are going to meet at a coffee shop, during the day. You lost your privileges to just come and go as you wish from my house."

Her scowl says she's dead serious.

"Right. Yeah, of course," I say, hedging. "You're right. I have to work tomorrow, though. How about the day after?"

"I'm busy all day Wednesday," she says in a flat voice. "When's your next day off?"

"I have Thursday morning free," I say with a shrug.

"Fine. Let's meet at ten?" She glances around restlessly, clearly ready to go.

"Ten is perfect." Ten is terrible for me, actually. I planned on surfing all morning, but I don't tell Emma that. "Can I bring anything?"

"Just bring your books. I'll text you the location."

On the tip of my tongue is a question about why the fuck she hasn't answered any of my 'just checking in' texts. I bite back my questions, though.

"Okay. Great—"

She's already turning back to her shopping cart, ready to leave.

"Emma, wait…" I say.

Her dark head turns, and she looks at me, disinterest in her green gaze. "Yes?"

Nothing has ever cut me so deep, so fast. I suck in a breath, exhaling my response. "Thanks."

She rolls her eyes, grabbing her cart and heading to the front of the store. I watch her walk away, the hem of her sundress sliding against the back of her thighs.

Fuck! Stupid! I silently curse myself.

I caused this. I did it for the sake of Asher's friendship, but it still hurts like hell.

I amble back to my own shopping cart, feeling like I just got ran over by a fucking Mack truck. I glance back, but Emma is gone.

Leaning my elbows on the cart, I putter around, not wanting

to crowd her by going up to the register while she's still waiting in line to check out. I stop for a second, and scrub a hand over my facial hair.

I know that it's better this way. I had to break up with her. Asher would have found out, sooner or later... and his friendship means everything to me.

So I'm willing to suffer in silence. But I still want Emma in my life... even if it's just as a friend.

We can do that, I think. We can be friends.

Right?

4

EMMA

Why didn't I just tell Jameson no?

I keep turning that question over and over in my mind as I make the drive from my house to the little coffee shop on the beach where I like to study.

Why am I such a sucker?

I know the answer, though. As soon as Jameson started toward me, in the aisle of the grocery store, I was pinned in place. Frozen, because I thought for the briefest second that he was about to ask me to take him back.

I swallow at the painful memory of feeling so weak around him, so easily destructible… if Jameson had only breathed a word about wanting me back, I don't know how I would have said no. He burned me, and treated me badly, and yet I would've jumped at the chance to do it all again.

How pathetic am I?

Luckily, Jameson only wanted me for my brain. That's my freaking life story, right there. He begged me to help him study for his GED, and like an idiot, I agreed.

I am so, so stupid. Stupid and pathetic.

I pull my coupe into a spot outside the coffee shop. Checking the time, I realize that I'm a little early for our meeting. I grab my purse and head inside the little shop, smiling at how comfy it is in here. From the mismatched secondhand couches to the eclectic art on the walls, the place just screams 'hang out forever' to me.

Heading to the counter, I make note of their aged espresso machine and young, hip staff. The girl who comes to help me is a young Latina woman, wearing high waisted denim shorts and what looks like a black ballet leotard.

"Hey," she says, nodding to me. She adjusts some of the plates of scones and muffins under the counter, not rushing me.

"Hey. Can I get a small latte? And…" I bend over to inspect the pastries. "What's good?"

"Mmm… I like the gluten free pop tarts," she says, pointing them out. "They're really good, for being gluten free."

"Alright, I'll try one." I smile at her as she rings me up, pay with a card, and then look around for a table.

I end up selecting one of the bar tables in the far corner, feeling like choosing a couch to sit on would really send the wrong message. I grab my latte and my pop tart, then sit on one of the high backed chairs.

As I eat my crumbly pastry and wait for Jameson to appear, I look around. The walls are painted dark purple, and there is art everywhere. I look out the huge bay window to my left, and see Jameson heading inside. He's silhouetted against the backdrop of the beach.

Dark hair, a few days growth over his chin and cheeks, tall and broad. I swallow when I realize he is wearing his leather motorcycle jacket and black jeans. Seeing him in that jacket makes me *yearn*.

He's still so gorgeous that just being near him makes me shake a little bit. He comes in, spots me, and heads over.

"Hey," he says, putting his backpack down. "Oh, you already got something. I was going to buy whatever you got, since you're helping me out."

I shrug. "It's fine."

He looks nonplussed. "Okay, let me get something. Then we can get started."

I drum my fingers as he heads up to the counter. As he waits in line, I blush a little to think of how I have to beg Evie to talk about her job, in hopes that a little news about Jameson will come up. When it does, I quiz her as casually as I can, but she sees right through me.

Another tiny bit of shame in my day. I can brush it off now, but later when I'm lying in my bed alone, I will remember this.

Jameson comes back with a cold brew coffee, sipping it as he takes the seat next to me. I realize as I am sitting here, staring at his throat when he swallows some of the coffee, at his long fingers as he places his glass on the table...

I may hate Jameson right now. I may be angry about the way he ended things with me. I might even have spent some time imagining him getting hit by a bus.

But none of that changes the fact that I am still drawn to Jameson, as much now as ever. And I hate myself for it.

He pulls a stack of books out of his bag and clears his throat. "You doing okay?"

I must be giving him a weird look or something. I quickly straighten my spine and blink away my thoughts.

"Fine," I say, trying not to snap at him. I nod toward the books. "What are we studying today?"

His brow hunches.

"Same as before. I thought we could start with math, and then do science."

"Right. Uh... I guess let me come over to your side of the table," he says. Sliding his books over, he takes his time to settle into the chair on my left. He moves his coffee over, and then opens his math textbook.

It's cold enough in this coffee shop that I can actually feel the heat radiating off of his big body. I bite my lower lip, rebuking myself for being so weak when it comes to him.

"So, I left off here, with differential equations..." he says, pointing to the section in the book. "But I wasn't sure about how they worked. Like, I can look at the examples all day long, but when a problem is in front of me, my mind goes blank."

"Ahhh." I nod, toying with my mug. "I think you need to see it in action. Do you have some paper?"

"Sure, yeah." He grabs a few sheets of blank paper out of his backpack, along with a pen. He slides them in front of me. "Here."

He cracks his knuckles. I swallow, trying not to listen to the voice inside my head that remembers all too well what those hands can do. How much pleasure they can wring out of my body, for hours on end.

"Okay... let's see... first you need to find the integer..." I say. I guide him through the process, doing several different problems.

Jameson hunches over the table, watching me work. He's making me nervous, but I refuse to let it show. I just don't look him in the eye, focusing instead on the paper and pen.

He asks a couple of questions, stopping me with a hand on my forearm. His warm fingers touch the bare skin of my wrist the second time, and my pulse jumps like a scared rabbit.

He glances at me, but I just move my arm away, clear my throat, and continue.

"I think I get it. Or at least, I understand enough to take the GED," he says.

I glance up at him, meeting his warm chocolate gaze. For the barest second, I am lost in his eyes, falling deep into them. He doesn't break the connection, either.

He just stares at me for a few seconds. I can tell there is something that he wants to say, but he doesn't say anything. And I'm too much of a chicken to ask him what he's thinking.

I avert my gaze. "Umm, do you think we should study science now?"

Clearing his throat, he nods. "Yeah. Uh... yeah. I'm studying physical science now, figuring out velocity and speed. It's... challenging."

"Great," I say, with forced cheer. Inside, I'm thinking that I wish I hadn't agreed to even come here. But I don't want him to know that. "Velocity it is!"

Jameson slides me a suspicious look as he gets out his science textbook. He opens it, but splays his hand over the page.

"Are you okay?"

His black-brown eyes search my face.

"Always," I counter, tapping the textbook to draw his attention back there. "Come on, let's study the basics of physics."

I brush his hand out of the way and begin reading. He eventually switches his focus to what we're reading. I stop several times, expelling the dynamics of what we are talking about more in depth. He listens and nods, asking a question here and there.

We go through the important bits of velocity and speed, and then I walk him through some of the mathematical equations that the book offers. I have him do a few sample problems.

At one point, when he's bent over the paper and scrawling out his answer, I sigh. It is a sort of longing sound, totally accidental and not really provoked by any one particular thing.

It's just Jameson, as a whole. Watching him do anything is pretty pleasurable, but watching him learn something new? Something that I can help him with?

It's almost swoon-worthy. So I sigh.

He looks up at me, and I turn pink. Busted.

"What?" he asks.

"Nothing," I respond, shaking my head. "Nothing, go on."

"You're being weird," he says.

"No, I'm not." I take a sip of my latte, as if that will save me from my own awkwardness.

"You are!" he insists. He puts the pen down. "Why are you being weird?"

"Jameson—" I start, annoyed that we're even having this conversation.

He gives me a hard look. I squirm a little bit in my chair. He drops his voice.

"You know, just because we're not fucking each other anymore, that doesn't mean you can't talk to me. I'm still the same person."

My face turns scarlet in an instant. "Jameson, you just… you are not following the proper breakup protocol in the least."

His eyebrows rise. "There is a protocol?"

I scowl. "Yes! And you are just like… walking all over it, like it's not even a thing. But trust me, it exists for a reason."

"The protocol?"

"Yes!"

There is a second where he pauses. I can see him doing some kind of calculation, and coming up frustratingly short.

"I guess I don't know what the rules are, when you're… you know, not seeing each other any more," he admits.

"Well, that's obvious." I feel like a grouch when I say it, but it's true.

"What is it that you want me to do, then?"

He looks at me, his face as serious as death. I deflate like a balloon under his gaze.

"I don't know. I mean…" I look down at my hands. "It just feels like… like nothing has changed."

My eyes mist over unexpectedly, and I'm beyond embarrassed.

"That's a good thing, right?" he asks.

"No!" I cry, louder than I intend. The barista looks over at me, and I cringe. But even so, I can't stop myself from talking. "You don't understand, Jameson. You— you broke my heart!"

He freezes in place, his face shocked. "I— I mean, I didn't mean to, Emma. I swear."

He reaches out to touch my hand, and I yank my hand off the table. Standing up, angry and hurt, I start to leave.

"Whoa, whoa, Emma," Jameson says, jumping up and blocking my exit with his big body. "Just wait a second."

My eyes are brimming with unshed tears. My voice is barely above a whisper. "Let me go."

"I'm sorry," he says. "I really am. Everything was my fault, okay?"

"It's not okay! I'm here, even though I don't want to be, doing you a favor. And you're invading my space and blocking me from leaving…"

One tear breaks free, snaking its way down my cheek unchecked. His expression is anguished.

"Don't cry. Please don't," he pleads with me. "I'll try to follow the rules, okay? Anything you say, I'll do."

I brush the tear from my cheek, taking a deep breath. His guilty expression twists at my heart. Now I feel bad for making him feel bad.

"Let me think about it. I… I want to tutor you, like it was before, but…" I shake my head, looking down. "I'm still hurting."

"I'll give you time, if that's what you need," he says. "Just… please don't say you can't see me anymore, socially."

I look up at him. "I said I'll think about it. That's all I can give you right now."

He sighs and shrugs a shoulder. "That's all I can ask, then."

He moves back, letting me go. I get out of there as quickly as possible, practically running past the barista and out the front door. I don't slow down until I get to my car.

I slide behind the wheel, my heart pounding.

I don't know if I can see him again.

But at the same time, how can I refuse?

I throw my car into drive and pull out, tires squealing.

5

JAMESON

I climb out of my Jeep at the diner that my brother Forest suggested. Shading my eyes against the midday sun, I wish that I hadn't had that last drink the night before. I'm definitely hungover.

I adjust my Ray-Ban sunglasses and head into the diner. The place is a little greasy spoon that Forest loves, painted bright orange inside and out. We eat here from time to time, but the owner always remembers us.

"Jameson!" she howls when I step inside. She's manning the grill, wearing her usual all-black outfit, and grinning ear to ear.

"Hey there Ms. Parker," I say with a nod.

I'm not even concerned about the fact that she got my name a little bit wrong. The fact is, she remembers almost everybody that comes in here, and that's pretty fucking impressive.

Ms. Parker points to the booth in the far corner, where Forest is already sitting. I give her a wave and head over there, sliding into there booth opposite my brother.

"Yo," I greet him. "What's up?"

Forest sips his coffee, then makes a contented sound. "Not much."

The waitress comes over, and I order a coffee and their

crawfish etouffee omelet. Forest orders french fries and scrambled eggs.

As I add some sugar to my black coffee, I study my brother. He has been to the barber recently, because his hair is cropped very close to his scalp. Always way more preppy than I've ever been, even today on his day off he has shaved.

"How are my investments doing, oh magical money maker?" I kid.

He considers that for a second. "Good. Actually, that's part of what I want to talk to you about."

"Oh yeah?" I ask. I sip my coffee. It's thick and black, just the way I like it.

"Yeah. You know how the apartment you and Asher live in is a duplex?"

"Mmm, I think the other side is full of... I don't know, the owner's stuff." The owner is an older man in his seventies, and he doesn't come around much these days.

"Well, Asher put out a feeler, just to see if the owner would be interested in selling him the place."

"Really?" I'm a little surprised that Asher didn't tell me about it, being that I'm supposedly his roommate and best friend.

"Yep. He just heard back, and the landlord is more than happy to get it off his hands."

"Huh." I consider that.

"My point in telling you this is that I think you and Asher should go in on the house together. Then you can each live in one half, or rent it out, or whatever you want to do. The place is a steal, only like $200,000. Split two ways, that's really really reasonable."

"Huh," I say again. I drum my fingertips on the laminate countertop. "Can I afford that?"

"Easily. And it will build equity for you too. I think it's a really solid idea."

"Cool," I say with a shrug. "Yeah, why not?"

"Well, I just want to make sure that there's nothing weird

between you guys before I bring the idea up to him. I mean, it's almost a no-brainer for you."

I give him a slow nod, thinking about Emma. She would definitely qualify as 'something weird" between me and Asher, but Asher doesn't know about it. I broke it off because of Asher, because of how he would act if he ever found out.

I sigh. "Yeah, there is nothing weird between us."

At least not anymore.

"Well, I figure that you'll eventually settle on one girl. And rumor has it, girls don't love their men to have roommates, even if they're as close as you guys are."

I raise an eyebrow. "Is that a statement about your personal life?"

Forest scowls. "No."

"Are you sure? Because I could see Addison giving you all kinds of shit over the fact that you still live with Gunnar. I imagine a girl like Addison, who's obviously from money, doesn't love your current living arrangements."

There are a few seconds of silence, when Forest looks at his coffee cup. I was mostly kidding, but clearly I've accidentally touched a nerve.

"I don't like your lack of response. What's up with you? Are things okay with you and Addison?" I ask after a minute.

Forest looks up at me, a note of pain shining in his eyes. "It's nothing."

"Bullshit. What's going on?"

Forest opens his mouth, but the waitress arrives with our plates just then. She sets down my omelet and Forest's eggs and fries, then refills our coffee.

"Do you guys need anything else?" she asks.

"No thanks," I say, trying not to let my impatience show. As soon as she's gone, I turn my attention back to Forest. "Spill."

He rolls his eyes. "I'm sure it's not even a thing."

I pick up my fork, intending to dig into my still-steaming omelet. "It's enough of a thing to worry you, obviously."

I take a bite of my food, burning my mouth a little. It's so good, though. I reach for the hot sauce, to slather on my food indiscriminately.

"Okay, okay. Addy's parents... they are not normal people. You know that they're super rich, houses in Beverly Hills and Aspen, all that jazz. They're super wealthy and connected."

I raise a brow. "I don't know them, but I definitely get a little rich girl vibe from Addison."

"Well, they definitely don't like me. I found out this week that Mr. Montgomery only said yes when I asked for his blessing because Addy threatened him."

I pause with a forkful of food in front of my face.

"Wait, why don't they like you?" I'm a little baffled by this.

"As it turns out, Addy apparently told them that I'm not from the best circumstances, family wise. In the year we were dating, before I met them, she told them all about my tragic past, I guess. She's so fucking melodramatic."

He punctuates that statement by shoving several french fries into his mouth. I frown at him.

"Well that's shitty. What are you supposed to do about it?"

He shakes his head. "I mean, there's nothing I can do about it, I don't think. And every time I talk about the wedding now, Addy gives me this look. Like... if I were a paranoid guy, I would say it's a knowing look. She has something planned, or something she isn't telling me."

I pause. "Like what?"

"I don't know, man. I just get some really negative energy, flowing from her to me."

"You think she's going to call off the wedding?"

He takes a second to eat some of his eggs, thinking that over. "I don't know. It's just bugging me. Like an itch that I can't scratch, that won't go away."

I nod, finishing my last bite of food. I sip my coffee, thinking it over. "What are you going to do about it?"

Forest shrugs. "Probably nothing. I've asked her about it, a few times. She says nothing is wrong."

"Well, I am maybe not the best source of advice on this. Everyone knows that I'm fucking dumb—"

"Don't say that," he says with a frown.

"Seriously? Anyway—"

"I'm dead serious. You're one of the smartest people I know."

"*Anyway*," I say, deliberately talking over him. "If something feels off, it probably is. I don't think it's weird that you're worried about it."

He sighs, pushing his plate away. "Thanks, dude. It is kind of nice, knowing that you think so too."

That wasn't what I said, exactly, but I let it go. I finish my quickly cooling cup of coffee, and the waitress comes by with a coffee pot for a refill.

"So… since this has turned into brotherly bonding time…" Forest says.

I look up at him, curious. "Yeah?"

"Are you gonna tell me who the girl is that dumped you?"

I glower at him. "Who says there's a girl?"

"I've been watching you at work lately. You're all distracted, and you're in a bad mood half the time. That's after like a straight month of easy, breezy *especially* carefree Jameson. I would have to be blind not to notice that something was up."

"Girls come and go," I hedge. "You know that."

"I'm just saying, since you were all blissed out for a while there, maybe she turned your head the right way. You should consider the power that begging has in any situation."

He sips his coffee. I wad up a paper napkin and throw it at him.

"That's for assuming that it was my fault," I intone.

"Ah! So there was a girl. I knew it!" He grins. "Was it someone I know?"

"Like I'm going to tell you."

He squints at me for a long second. "It's not Maia, is it?"

"What? No. You and Gunnar are so damn obsessed with her, it's not even funny."

"She's hot!" he says defensively.

"All right, Mr. Is My Fiancée Cheating On Me."

He glares at me. "Don't turn this around on me. We're talking about you."

"Are we talking about why you assume that she dumped me? Because I want you to know, I was the one who did the breaking up."

"Yeah, normally I would believe that, but you were so happy when you were with the mystery girl. So if you did do the breaking up, it was because you had to. Like, you were forced to do it."

I look down at my coffee mug. He hit way too close to home. "Maybe I just didn't like her that much."

"To quote you, bullshit. I'm looking at you right now, and you can't even look at me when you say that."

I give him my surliest look. "So what?"

"So what? So I'm saying, if you're really so hung up on this girl, apologize for whatever you did." I start to argue, but he puts a hand up, stopping me. "Don't even bother trying to tell me that you didn't do something worth apologizing over. I've been watching a lot of The Bachelorette, because that's Addy's favorite TV show. The guy is always the one that is in the wrong. Every single time."

"You're so full of shit," I say, reaching for my wallet. I pull out two twenties, dropping them on the table. "Excuse me for not taking advice from you, okay? I still remember when you were thirteen and you kept getting in trouble for drawing naked women in the bathrooms at school, okay? I think I'm good on advice from you."

Forest rolls his eyes. "It's been literally eighteen years since that happened. Are you ever going to let that go?"

"Fat chance." I slide out of the booth, ready to go.

Forest talks about needing to order some more cases of

whiskey while we walk out of the restaurant, but I'm not really paying attention.

Because of course Forest is right. Way more right than he knows. I really ripped out Emma's heart and trampled over it, because I knew Asher would find out.

And I couldn't risk losing my best friend.

But if Asher were suddenly erased, just gone? I would be on my knees, pleading with Emma to take me back.

I sigh and follow Forest out into the bright light of midday.

6

EMMA

I touch up my lipstick in the mirror of my bedroom at my parents' house, staring at my reflection. I'm wearing a gorgeous baby pink minidress, accented with a diamond necklace and earrings. My hair is in a braided updo, with a couple of pieces of hair strategically left hanging down in the front.

All that I'd need to add is a tiara, and I would be a perfect princess...

I sigh. My parents would love it if I dated someone who was royalty. They would rub it in the faces of their society friends at every opportunity.

That's the way the Alderisis were. They had raised me and Asher to be their prize jewels, and they were not above using pressure if they really needed us to shine.

Of course, Asher stopped accepting their money and their weird rich people guilt trips a long time ago. If only I could do the same... but I can't, at least until law school is over.

If Asher were here, he would make a joke about how dressed up I was. He'd make me laugh, at least.

Too bad Asher is kind of on my list of least favorite humans right now. Well, that and there's the fact that he wouldn't be caught dead celebrating my parents tonight.

There's a knock on my door, and my mom opens it. The sound of voices and piano music reach my ears; the party must have started.

"Are you ready, Emmaline?"

I turn and look at my mother, who is wearing a silver sequined gown. She's also absolutely dripping with diamonds. I force a smile at her and grab my clutch.

"I am. Happy anniversary, by the way."

My mother bows her head for a moment, her version of accepting the compliment. "Come, your father is waiting."

I leave behind my bedroom, still as pink and pristine as ever, and walk down the hall with my mother. The sounds of talking and the clattering of glassware grow louder as we approach the main staircase.

I let my mother go first, placing my left hand on the bannister, my heels clicking against the marble underfoot. We smoothly descend the stairs in perfectly synchronized movements, a lifetime of practice in plain view for everyone to see.

As we reach the bottom of the stairs, they open up into a sort of rotunda, which feeds into what my mother calls the *entertaining floor*. A game room, a huge dining room, a living room type area with big verandah doors thrown wide open. There is even a kitchen tucked away in the back, to prepare food for parties like this one.

The fact that my parents even have a floor just for entertaining guests is beyond snooty. I repress a sigh, preparing myself for a whole night of talking to people who take my parents' wealth in stride.

"Leslie, there you are!" a woman in a red evening dress says. "Oh, you had little Emma come home from college! That's wonderful."

"Karen," my mother says, greeting her with a nod.

I slip on my mask, smiling benevolently. My mother greets Karen, and Karen gives me a quick peck on the cheek.

"Karen, I have to settle my daughter in for moment." My mother's gaze flicks to me. "She's hardly ever at home. Isn't that right, Emmaline?"

I smile. "It is."

"Come find me after that," Karen says. She leans in conspiratorially. "You won't believe what I heard about Megan Denning. D-I-V-O-R-C-E."

My mother inclines her head and leads me onward. We walk down a walkway that divides the game room and dining room, and head into the living room. There are tons of brown leather couches artfully arranged here and there, with cream shag rugs and a small library against one wall.

My father is there, leaning on the library ladder, a beautiful leather-bound volume in one hand. He's taller than most of the men who are circled around him, listening to him… well, he's orating, if I were to be honest.

Standing in a circle in their tuxes, they resemble nothing so much as a bunch of confused penguins. I stifle a grin.

I notice that the men he has chosen to surround himself with are much younger, the sons of oil executives and foreign shipping barons. My eyes narrow; Alan Alderisi normally wouldn't have anything to do with a bunch of young guys like this.

Before I can put two and two together, my mother calls to my father. "Alan, dear, look who has finally come down!"

Eight sets of eyes turn to me. Suddenly, I'm in a spotlight of my parents' creation. I want to turn and run, but my mother's hand lands on my forearm. Her grip is as firm as steel.

"Emma," my father says, urging me to step forward. "I was just telling some of your contemporaries here a story about when I was their age. Come, come meet the gentlemen…"

I have never felt like such a piece of meat as I do now, with seven strange men staring at me, expectation evident in their eyes. I move forward into the opening of the circle, trying to keep a smile on my face. I am red as a beet, I'm sure of it.

"Hi," I say, folding my hands together. "Nice to meet you all, I'm sure."

They introduce themselves, their names going right over my head. The final guy is a tall, lanky blond in an expensive-looking tuxedo. He elbows aside the suitors on either side of himself, eager to make an impression. I look at him, all swagger and no actual grit, and I instantly dislike him.

He grabs my hand, pressing it in his clammy grip. "Emma, I'm Rich. May I just say how beautiful you are?"

I want to rip my hand back, but I don't. Instead I just give him a vague smile and incline my head. It's a page straight out of my mother's playbook.

Rich seems unaware of how weird it is. Not that I really want to talk to any of them, but what about the six guys left staring at me? He pulls my hand into the crook of his arm, turning his back on the whole group. "I think we should take a walk."

I turn too, in an effort not to let him crush my hand. I throw an alarmed look over my shoulder to my father, but he's already wandered off.

"If you don't mind—" I start.

"Come on, let's go outside," Rich says, undeterred. I'm honestly not sure whether my reaction even registers with him. "Your father says you're in law school. That must be difficult."

"Uhhh... yes?" is all I can come up with.

He steers me out of the living room, past the broad terrace doors, and down the brick steps toward the expansive gardens. The sun is still out, which is the only reason why I'm even letting this happen.

When the sun goes down, I had damn well better be back inside. I scowl, but Rich is so self-involved that he doesn't even notice.

"I thought about going to law school, but I decided to get my

MBA instead. I went to Wharton, of course. And Harvard before that…"

He launches into his entire life history, really taking the time to explain his pedigree to me. His story is long, winding, and dead boring. I lose interest in it pretty quickly. I focus on the flowers in bloom as we walk along the garden path.

As we walk, Rich gesticulates to emphasize what he is saying. His hand catches my eye, and I realize that he has a manicure. And not a subtle one, either… he actually has a coat of clear polish on his nails.

While I try not to judge, that detail emphasizes to me how ridiculous letting my parents set me up is. Asher and Jameson would *hate* Rich for being so foppish, that's for sure.

If I'm honest, this is all starting to feel very much like a long lost plot arc of Pride and Prejudice. I imagine myself dressed in period costume, walking in the gardens with one of my many suitors. Yeah, it's a little too much like real life for my tastes.

"So what about you?" Rich asks.

Oh, he's asking me a question. I flush, because I have not been paying enough attention to answer.

"Er… what do you mean?" I ask.

He looks down his nose at me, squeezing my arm pityingly. "I mean, you're a dazzling girl. But I want to know all of your schools, your history, etc. You can't hope to just get a husband by merit of your parents name, I would think."

I arch my brows. "I wasn't aware that I was trying to get a husband."

He rolls his eyes at me. "We're all looking to partner up. I just want to make the best possible match for myself, which is why I ask about your background."

Stopping short, I pull my arm from his grip. I raise my hand, shading my eyes from the sun. "I'm not really worried about your wants and needs, honestly. I'm here because my parents want me to be at their party."

"Yeah, but—" he starts to explain.

"Yeah, no," I say, shaking my head. "I'm going back to the house now."

I turn and start to walk back. He catches up to my in two long strides.

"Wait, wait," he says. "This isn't going how I planned at all."

"Oh?" I keep walking, refusing to slow down.

"I just… I think you're very beautiful—"

"That is not a good reason to try to date someone," I say.

"Well, you're also smart, and you come from the right sort of family—"

I stop short again, whirling to face him. He sees the irate look on my face, and backs up a couple of inches.

"You don't know anything about me, other than who my father is. You're jumping ahead to whether or not you and I fit into your compatibility matrix before you even know anything about me!"

"I'm just being practical," Rich defends. "I don't want to waste my time, or yours."

"This is why I don't let my parents set me up," I say, throwing my hands up. "Now if you don't mind, I'm going to go for a walk. *Alone.*"

He looks nonplussed, but I don't really care. I'm pissed at my parents, pissed at this whole elite little world that they've created for me. It's enraging, being stuck in the hamster wheel that they invented.

I veer off the path, heading toward the guest house. I need to cool down a little bit, without being bombarded by my mother or any of the would-be suitors.

The path grows more lush as I continue on, verdant trees cropping up as I reach the edge of our property. Though I'm headed for the guest house, I slow as I approach my favorite spot in the gardens.

A little clearing leads up to the oldest oak tree on the property. It's massive, its branches spanning out at least ten feet on each side. In front of the trees, there is a little concrete bench. Nothing fancy, just a good spot for contemplation.

I walk to the bench and sit down with a sigh. This bench has seen a lot, and the tree has seen even more in its life.

I start thinking of Asher and Jameson, of how long their friendship has been. It's almost noble, Jameson giving up whatever could have been between us to avoid hurting Asher. I mean, it still sucks, but it's almost understandable.

I lapse into daydreaming, the party a mere echo in the far distance.

7

EMMA

Six Years Earlier

"I promise you, you're going to meet so many cute guys tonight," my friend Candace whispers in my ear. "Plus I heard that there are going to be older guys there. Like they've already graduated and they have jobs and stuff. Can you believe it?"

She says it like we've won some kind of prize. I giggle as she pulls me down the sidewalk in a neighborhood near Stanford. We're dressed to the nines and already a little tipsy.

I hear the party raging before we even see the house that it's at. The house is modest at best, a little grey shack that's barely big enough to hold two bedrooms. Loud music is pumping full-blast out of a pair of giant speakers in the yard; there are tons of people standing and talking over the obnoxiously loud music, and a few girls are dancing.

"See? What'd I tell you?" Candace says, squeezing my arm hard. "The real party is inside, though."

I take her hand as we head up the driveway and squeeze between people to get to the front door. Inside is even more packed, with people having conversations while other people shimmy around them, heading for the front or back door.

"Tammy!!" Candace screams.

A pretty blonde head turns around. Tammy's eyes widen, and she squeals with excitement. "Girls! You're here!!"

We work our way over to where Tammy is, Candace throwing a couple of elbows here and there. I notice that Tammy is standing by a plastic table, which is a sort of makeshift bar. At least, there are twenty different bottles of cheap liquor on it, and another half dozen bottles of soft drinks.

When we get to Tammy, she already has shots lined up for us in red solo cups.

"Here, bitches!" she shouts, handing us each a solo cup.

I look at the purplish liquid in the bottom of the cup a little suspiciously. "What is it?"

"Don't ask questions, silly!" Tammy says. "Just cheers!"

She and Candace toast, so I do too. Then we drink. I wince at the sugariness of it; I think that it is literally vodka with Kool-Aid mix and a ton of sugar.

"Amazing!" Candace says. "You're the best bartender, Tammy."

Tammy grins. "Come on, come to the back yard. They have an ice block set up back there to do shots!"

"Omigod, really?" Candace shrieks.

I sigh, tagging along behind them. If I weren't so petrified to meet guys alone, I would never even be here. But I am here, so I go along with whatever they want to do.

For the next two hours, I do shots, play beer pong, and try my hand at some card game that everyone seems to know called Kings and Assholes.

About an hour in, things get a little blurry around the edges. I blearily try to count how many drinks I've had, but I can't. My friends are getting sloppy drunk, and apparently so am I.

We get friendly with a group of guys that Candace knows from high school. Candace makes out with one of them quite extensively. Then two hours in, Candace runs outside to puke in the bushes. I go with her, trying to clean up, but the guy that she made out with shoos me away.

"She gets like this sometimes," he says with a shrug. "I'll take her home. No funny business, I swear."

He half-drags her out of the party. I look around for Tammy, but she's mysteriously missing.

God damnit. Now I'm drunk and alone.

One of the guys that Candace introduced me to, Brad, comes over and puts his arm around me. A red light goes off in my drunk brain. I need to get the hell out of here, now.

Thumbing through my phone, I slip outside and sit down in the trampled grass. I call Asher first, but his phone just rings until his voicemail picks up.

After a few tries, I scowl at my phone. "Jerk."

I scroll through the other contacts, stopping on Jameson. Figuring that it's worth a try, I call him. I don't actually expect him to pick up.

Except, he does. The phone rings twice, then an out of breath Jameson answers.

"Hello?"

"Oh!" I say. "You picked up the phone."

There's a second of hesitation on his part, and the murmur of another voice in the background. I can't hear what is said, but the timbre says it's a woman.

"Hold on." I hear noise, like the phone is being moved around. "Emma? You okay?"

"I'm at a party," I say. Then, unsure if I'm slurring or not, I say, "I think... I think I need a ride. Asher's not answering his phone."

I hiccup, ending the statement there.

"Shit," Jameson says. "Uhhh.... alright. Where are you?"

"I'm at..." I turn, squinting at the house. "704 Sycamore Drive."

"Alright. Are you somewhere safe for now? Can you hang out for ten or fifteen minutes until I can get there?"

"Yep," I say, then hiccup again. "I'm great."

"Okay. Don't move. I'll be right there."

I grin as the phone line goes dead. Jameson is coming here, right now. He's going to pick me up!

I'm absurdly happy about that. I sit and wait, happily drunk.

"Hey there," a strange guy says. He's only a few feet away, wearing all black. "What are you doing over here by yourself?"

I squint at him. I'm pretty sure that he is way too old to be at this party.

"Who are you?" I ask. "You don't look like you should be here."

He chuckles, coming closer. "Don't worry about that part. What's your name?"

I frown at him. "I don't like you. Go away."

He squats down next to me. From this distance, I can smell the sour beer on his breath, taste the heavy cologne he has doused himself with.

He reaches out his hand, as if to stroke my face. Wincing, I manage to crab walk backwards, avoiding his touch. His smile only grows wider.

"You're being very naughty," he says, tsking. "Someone ought to teach you some manners. Maybe that someone should be me."

"Get away from me," I say, shaken by his words. I try to stand up, failing the first time. "I don't want you to talk to me."

"You're pretty drunk. Let me help you home," he says. "We wouldn't want anything bad to happen to you."

Out of nowhere, Jameson appears in the yard. He takes one look at the situation — me standing shakily, the guy approaching me with a grin — and rushes in between us.

"Get the fuck away from her," Jameson growls. Next to Jameson, the other guy seems tiny and unthreatening.

"Whoa," the guy says, putting up his hands. "I didn't realize she was spoken for."

That seems to set Jameson off. He lunges forward, grabbing the guy by the shirt.

"You don't treat people like that," Jameson grits out, shaking the other guy. "If someone says to leave them alone, you do it."

"Alright!" the guy says, his voice going up a few scales. "Let me go, man."

Jameson pushes the guy away. "You need to leave. I don't want to see you around here again. Comprende?"

"Fuck off," the other guy says, but he's already moving away, across the yard.

I am standing there, shaken and grateful. Jameson looks at me.

"Are you okay?" he asks.

"Mmmhm." I want to throw myself on him and thank him. I want to kiss him, or maybe tell him that I love him. But suddenly, I feel a little sick.

I look at him, my eyes watering, my mouth filling with that kind of spit that tells you you are definitely going to throw up.

"Let's get you to the car, okay?" Jameson comes closer, but I throw a warning arm up...

And then vomit on his Converse. He jumps back. "Fuck."

I want to apologize, but apparently I'm not done. I run over to the bushes and wretch a few times, throwing up bright purple liquid. That is definitely alarming.

I am beyond ashamed. Not only am I vomiting, but I'm doing it in front of the one guy that I've been dreaming about since I was fifteen years old. That thought is never far from the surface, tangled up with everything else that is going on in my brain.

Jameson comes over and pulls my hair out of my face, and rubs my back until I'm done. I think he murmurs something soothing, telling me it's going to be okay, but I'm really wrapped up in the business of throwing up.

When I'm done, Jameson guides me to his car and gets me inside. I slump against the door as he drives me back to his house that he shares with Asher, ashamed, exhausted, and drunk.

Jameson manages to get me into his house and to the couch

in his living room. I sprawl all over the place while Jameson takes my shoes off my feet and gets me a glass of water.

He covers me with a blanket and turns out the lights.

"I'm sorry," I slur, my eyes closing of their own volition.

I think I hear a smile in his voice, but I'm not sure. "Don't be."

"It's not how I thought tonight would go…" I whisper.

Then I fall asleep.

8

JAMESON

Current Day

I glance around the apartment, at the countless stacks of old newspapers, giant trash piles, and two piles of what looks like clothing. Every pile is overflowing, some so high that they nearly touch the ceiling. There is a path carved out among the piles of stuff, but I'm afraid to move too fast. It looks like it could all be set off into a miniature avalanche with one wrong move.

I lift a sheet of plywood up that was on top of a bunch of broken down dishwashers. Whatever is underneath smells pretty foul. I take a step back, wrinkling my nose.

"*Dude.*" Asher covers his mouth and coughs as dust flies everywhere. We're on the other side of our duplex, cleaning out the side used for storage."I literally think the landlord used to store actual junk here. And I think at some point he had animals."

I just grunt in acknowledgment. I hulk out, lifting the plywood overhead and carefully picking my way through the piles of broken computer parts and newspapers until I get outside. I set the plywood down on the porch, beside the other large pieces of junk that we've pulled out of the house.

It feels good to move around a little, after not doing anything too physically strenuous for a few days. My t-shirt is a little sweaty; I pull it away from my skin, giving myself a little air.

Asher joins me, handing me a bottle water. "What do you think?"

I look at him, twisting the cap on the water. "About what?"

"About the house. I mean, can you see this side being lived in, after we clean it out?"

I consider that for a minute, peering back inside. "Yeah. I mean, I think that the house has good bones. But there is just a ton of crap inside."

"Yeah. I'm thinking of backing my truck up here on the lawn so we can get rid of all those newspapers. The dishwashers, though…"

I lean against the house. "Anything that has to go to the dump, you can just pay to have it all hauled away by the regular trash guys. I think you just call them to arrange it."

"Hmm," he says, nodding. "Should we get a start on the newspapers?"

"Yeah. If you want to pull your truck up, I'll start moving stacks of them onto the porch."

"Word." He jumps off of the porch, and I head inside.

I grab a bunch of newspapers off of the nearest pile, hauling them outside. I glance at Asher, who is backing up his truck. He's been pretty quiet about where he's been recently, but he's definitely been somewhere other than here.

It's a little weird, because I feel like I've been here, hanging around. Waiting for Asher to confide in me again, like we used to in the old days.

I mean, I even broke things off with Emma, thinking that Asher would find out and be really upset. But of course, he hasn't even been around enough to find out anything…

He's been really self-involved lately. With Evie, apparently, according to his own drunk confession. I'm not sure that he even remembers his little drunk confession, or that he was heartbroken over Evie.

Something bad must have happened between them... but judging by the fact that Asher hung out for a couple weeks and then vanished, I would guess that it has been resolved.

I'm not mad about that, in itself. I'm just mad because I could be wrapped up in myself, wrapped up in Emma, if it wasn't for the friendship I have with Asher.

Basically now I'm left wondering if I overreacted and shot myself in the foot over something he doesn't even really care about. Asher gets out of the truck and lets the gate down, then heads up to the porch.

"Let me grab these really quick..." Asher says, moving the few stacks of newspapers I've already dragged out of the house into the truck.

Then we are both grabbing stacks of newspapers, hauling them outside, and tossing them into the back of the truck. For a while, I am happy enough to do it in silence, but after a bit I grow tired of the silence.

"Where have you been staying at for the last little while?" I ask, hauling a stack of newspaper up from the living room floor.

Asher falters a bit. "I didn't realize that you'd noticed."

I raise a brow. "You thought I wouldn't notice when you all but disappeared from the house that we both live in?"

"Right." He shakes his head. "I just sort of hoped that you would do what you always do, which is shack up with some surfer chick and not really pay as much attention to what I do."

I pause. "You think that's what I do?"

"I mean, yeah. That's been your M.O. for a few years."

I hadn't thought of it that way. "Alright, but aside from me. Why are you like... avoiding the house?"

He picks up a stack of newspapers, taking a moment to carry it outside and toss it. When he comes back, he wipes sweat from him brow.

"I'm not trying to. I just… I've been seeing this girl, and she is pretty obsessive about keeping things private."

"You mean Evie, right?"

He looks a me, clearly surprised. "How do you know it's Evie?"

I roll my eyes. "You told me when you were drunk. You called her a bitch, too."

Asher frowns. "I am such a traitor when I'm drunk. I really shouldn't have told you anything."

I give him a look. "Dude, I'm the best friend you've got in the world. You can tell me anything."

He looks away. "I know, but…"

I am more than a little offended. "What do you mean, but?"

He seems to realize that he has stepped into a no-go area. "Sorry. I just… I shouldn't talk about it."

I lift a pile of newspaper. "So that's it, then? We were best friends, until a girl came between us?"

"It's not like that. We're still best friends—"

My face contorts. "Except that your girl comes first. Is that right?"

"Not in so many words."

"This is bullshit," I bite off, heading back outside. I throw the papers into his truck, disgusted. With him, but also with myself.

Asher follows me onto the porch. "You'll understand when you meet the girl you're supposed to be with."

Emma flashes in my mind, first thing. I mean, Emma and I never got far enough for me to know for sure, but I'm still resentful as hell. I glare at him.

"And how do you know that I haven't?" I challenge.

"Dude, you would know. You wouldn't be able to shut up about it."

"Maybe I would be able to. Maybe I am just better at keeping my fucking mouth shut than you are."

He rolls his eyes at me. "You haven't dated anybody for long enough to have a horse in this race."

I clench my fists. If Asher was hoping to pick a fight today, mission accomplished.

"You don't know me," I say through gritted teeth. "You used to, but not anymore. You have no idea who I date, and no say either."

"No say?" He seems to find that part confusing.

I open my mouth to tell him everything, to spill my guts about Emma.

And his motherfucking phone rings. He glances at me, frowning, and pulls his phone out of his pocket.

"Shit," he mutters. He turns away from me, picking up. "Hello?"

He talks for a minute, periodically glancing back at me. Then he ends the call.

"That was Gunnar. There is something wrong with all of the coolers at Cure. They just aren't working."

"What? Why didn't he call me?"

Asher shrugs. "I don't know. But I have to go over to the bar for a while. I assume that we're going to need some kind of maintenance person to repair whatever's broken."

I narrow my eyes. "Uh huh."

"Come on, don't give me grief over this. We'll finish our conversation later."

I shrug. "No need. I feel like we've said all that there is to say, really."

I walk back into that wreck of a house, fuming.

"Jameson!" Asher calls.

But I'm done. Done with his self-involvement. Done pretending that we are best friends. He has been brutally honest about the fact that he considers Evie his best friend, anyway.

Most of all, I'm done with his bullshit rules.

Of course, it's a little too late for me to just go up to Emma and tell her. I feel like I'm sorry, I changed my mind isn't going to cut it.

But it's sort of freeing to know that in the future, I don't have to live by his rules anymore. The question is, what does a future without Asher's restrictive rules look like?

And why do I have trouble imagining any future with anyone but Emma?

9

EMMA

"Okay, but how do we feel about this? Do we think that it is just the right amount of over the top, or is it just overkill?" Maia asks, posing in the doorway of her living room. "I don't want to fall prey to my mother's instinct for over the top everything. She's from Hong Kong, so she's partially excused, but... you know."

I'm sitting on a low blue suede couch with pretty blonde Alice, eyeing Maia's outfit. It's a red lace jumpsuit, low cut in the front and back, and it emphasizes Maia's tiny waist.

"I think it's perfect," Alice says. "Very cutting edge."

"It's not too revealing, is it?" Maia asks, turning for us to inspect her. Her British accent makes me smile.

"No," I assure her. "You'll be the belle of the ball."

"Wonderful!" she says. "I mean, even though we are only going to Cure, I want to be sure that we all look posh."

I stand up, brushing off the skirt of my blue gingham minidress. "I think we might be making a mistake going to Cure. We're definitely hot enough to go anywhere."

Alice and Maia look at each other. Something secret passes between them, and they both supress smiles.

"Let's plan to start at Cure. Then if the party sucks, we'll go somewhere else," Alice suggests.

I raise my eyebrows, but I don't argue with them. Besides, it's not like I have a better idea.

"Alright, let's go then," Maia says, getting her phone out. "I'll call an Uber, so no one has to worry about what cars are where tomorrow morning."

We head out of the house. I follow Alice, carefully picking a spot of dark colored lint off of her strappy white dress. She smiles at me as we climb into the Uber.

"I'm so glad you finally agreed to come out with us," Alice says. "We were starting to worry about you."

Maia looks back at me from the front passenger seat, her expression mouth quirking. She knows that Jameson and I were a thing, but she's far too polite to ask what happened.

"Yeah, I don't know why I took so long," I say, glancing out the window at the darkened street. "It's not like I've been doing anything for the last month."

"Well you're here now, that's all that matters," says Maia. "And we're going to have a great freaking time tonight."

"Yes we are!" Alice cheers.

Soon enough we pull up to Cure and hop out of the car, thanking the driver. Maia is off like a shot, practically running to get in the door of the bar.

I look at Alice, raising my eyebrows at her in a questioning glance. She shrugs and rolls her eyes, and we both hurry to catch up to Maia.

As soon as Maia pulls the door open, the throb of the bass line vibrates the soles of my shoes. I step in the doorway behind Maia and A, my eyes adjusting to the room. It's dark in here, with plenty of fog and lasers.

It's also packed to the limit. It's only ten thirty, but the DJ that Gunnar has been talking up is apparently a huge draw. There are people everywhere, dancing and talking and listening to other people shouting.

"Wow," Alice shouts. "I did not expect this!"

Maia pushes her way through the crowd, and Alice and I follow her. On the way, I spot Brad awkwardly dancing with Gisella, grinning like an absolute idiot.

I stop and greet them for a minute, noting the way that Brad's hands never stray too far from Gisella's hips. I'm jealous of them for that. They both look deliriously happy, and I am jealous of that too.

When I say goodbye to them, my eyes automatically start to search for Jameson. The bar is so crowded that it takes a minute to suss him out.

But then I see him, tall and dark in his rolled up shirt sleeves, working silently but furiously behind the bar. When I get up to the bar, squeezing into the space that Maia has saved for me, he's got two cocktail shakers going at once.

He smoothly shakes them, and then pops them open, pouring their contents into glasses. It's nice to be able to see him like this, in his element. It's almost like it was before we ever kissed, when I would just watch him bartend like a lovestruck little girl.

I sigh, just as he looks up and makes eye contact with me. Jameson looks confused for a second, and then this ridiculous smirk takes over his whole face. I narrow my gaze at him.

"Here," Alice says, pressing a drink into my hands. I take it, turning my attention to the girls.

"To us!" Maia shouts, holding her champagne flute up. "May we live forever."

Alice and I clink our glasses to hers, and I sip mine. It's pretty good, all the fizziness of champagne with a little bit of... maybe chai flavor? Cinnamon and cardamom and all that jazz.

"Woo!" Alice cheers. "Let's get this party started!"

She turns to the bar, pointing at Forest. "Make us another round!!"

Forest flashes her a grin and does her bidding. I sip my champagne again, giggling when Maia puts her fingers on the stem of my glass, pushing it upward.

It forces me to drink a lot faster than I normally would, but I figure it's okay. I'm in about the safest place ever to get drunk, considering that Asher and Jameson own this place.

Glancing at Jameson again, I quickly finish my first drink. He makes eye contact with me again, and for a second, I swear that there is no one else in the room. Time slows. I take a step forward, almost forgetting why we aren't seeing each other anymore.

"Hey," Maia says, elbowing me in the ribs. "Will you please get your head in the game?"

"Huh?" I say, giving myself a shake. "What game?"

"We're going to all find a hot guy, and we are going to make out with them. That is the goal tonight." She gives me a mischievous grin.

"Here, have another drink," Alice says, taking my drink and replacing it with a fresh one. "After we finish this one, we can dance."

"You are both terrible influences." I drink a little champagne and giggle.

"We're just sick of boys telling us how to be," Maia says, shrugging one shoulder. "I personally am so sick of hearing about what men think."

"Cheers to that!" I say, toasting the girls.

We finish our drinks and then head out onto the dance floors. I feel great, as bubbly as champagne and as free as a bird. I dance with the girls, feeling myself, and have a great time. Someone eventually gets another round, and I drink that too.

I turn occasionally to glance at Jameson, not even pretending to be sly about it. Every time, he's already looking at me, his eyes glued on my figure.

Knowing that he just has to stand there and watch, and think about what he gave up when he dumped me… I admit, it sort of gives me life. It makes me dance harder and longer, with a secret smile on my face.

Eventually I notice that there's a tall guy dancing next to me. I make eye contact with him a few times, and he dances closer.

I shift, making my body language open, and before I know it we are dancing together. Not touching, yet, but dancing all the same.

"What's your name?" he shouts into my ear.

"I'm Emma!" I cry.

"Emma, I'm Jake! You're a good dancer!"

"Thanks!"

I bite my lip, placing my hands on Jake's shoulders. Jake grins and puts his hands on my waist, pulling me closer.

I lean close, noticing that he smells good. Kinda like sandalwood. And yeah, he's not as tall and brooding as Jameson, but Jake is hot in a goofy way. He is sort of lanky, but athletic. I peer up at him, trying to guess his age.

He's probably only a few years older than me, the appropriate age I guess. I study his shoes and his clothes, and decide that he isn't a member of my parents class.

That makes me like him way more, automatically. I get a glance at Jameson when Jake spins me in that direction. Jameson is scowling, beyond pissed. He looks like there should be a corresponding black thundercloud over his head.

I know it's beyond petty, but I'm glad. Glad that Jameson sees me dancing with another guy. Glad that I'm having fun with Jake. Glad that Jameson looks so friggin miserable.

Good, let him be angry and upset. That is how I've felt this whole time, ever since he broke up with me. It feels great to rub it in Jameson's face a little.

"Hey, do you—" Jake starts.

But he's cut off when I lift up onto my tiptoes and press my lips to his. I can see the surprise written on his face, but he catches on quickly enough.

Jake slides an arm around me, dipping me back a little bit. He's actually a surprisingly good kisser, and I open my mouth to him, inviting him to press further.

His tongue snakes against mine, sending a little shiver up my spine. I close my eyes, surrendering to the moment.

"Get out of the fucking way," I hear Jameson growl behind me. "Move!"

My eyes snap open as Jameson reaches me, snatching me away from Jake as easily as a rag doll.

"What the fuck?" Jake says, looking askance at J. "Let her go, dude."

"Get the fuck out of my bar," Jameson spits. "Now, before I make you get out. Trust me, you don't want to fuck with me."

"Jameson—" I say.

"You shut up," Jameson says to me. "I've heard enough from you tonight."

I look at Jake apologetically. "I'm sorry. Maybe it's better if you go…"

"Damn right," Jameson seethes. "Emma and I have some things to clear up, here."

"Jameson—"

Jameson hauls me up by the arm. "We need to talk in private."

I look at Jake, who seems to be trying to decide whether or not he should fight Jameson. "I'm fine, I promise."

Jameson forces me to start walking with him, out of the patio door and into the moonlight. There are a few bar patrons outside, so Jameson tows me off of the patio. We emerge into the alley where we almost had sex, and I shake off his grasp.

"Let *go*," I say, frowning at him. "What is wrong with you?"

He glowers at me, taking a step closer. He is huge; his physicality all sort of hits me at once. Jameson is just a big person. He could hurt me if he wanted to, really really badly.

He doesn't though. He just gets too close, intimidating me with his size.

"You can't come to my bar to meet strange men and think that I'm going to be fine with that," he rumbles.

I take a breath. I can feel his eyes on my body, feel his

weighted gaze, too hot in this dank little alley. I cross my arms to try to block his view a little.

"I should be able to do whatever I want to. See whomever I want to, wherever I want to. I don't know if you remember this or not, but *you* broke up with *me*."

He clenches his fists and leans towards me. "That's not fair. You know I didn't mean it like that."

I cock my head. "What does that even mean?"

He shoves his hand through his hair. "I mean, I broke up with you because of your brother. It doesn't mean that I don't..."

He trails off. I put my hands on my hips.

"What, that you don't have feelings for me? I thought I was just a fling. You seemed all too eager to throw that in my face before."

Jameson glances away. "Yeah, well. I was trying to do us both a favor."

I laugh. I can't help it, it just bubbles up.

"Save it. Whatever you are trying to do or say here, it doesn't matter."

"It does when it's happening in front of my face, at my bar!" he thunders.

I can't help the next bit, which comes out so loud that it leaves me shaken. "I didn't choose this, Jameson! You did! So live with it!"

"Emma— Emma, wait!" he tries.

But I'm not listening. I've had enough of Jameson and Asher and their bullshit.

Furious, I turn and fling myself down the alley, toward the parking lot. Tears blur my vision as I pull out my phone, searching for an Uber to take me out of this place.

10

EMMA

I'm hanging out at my house, which is starting to feel less like a place where two roommates live and more like a solo spot. Evie is still paying the measly five hundred bucks a month that is her share of the rent, but I haven't seen her in two weeks.

I've texted her a few times, asking when she would be back and inviting her to do stuff. She just texts back with vague excuses. I'm pretty sure she is going to move out soon. I'm bracing myself for it.

So I'm sitting in the mid-morning sun, reading an old copy of the Stanford Law Review on the front porch. I am thinking about food, vaguely dreaming of omelets.

I glance up to find Asher coming into the yard, a box of pastries and a couple cups of coffee balanced precariously in his arms. My eyebrows go up; I didn't expect him here.

"Evie isn't here," I call to him as he climbs the stairs to the porch. "I would've thought you'd know that, though."

He gives me a look. "I'm here to see you."

I'm instantly suspicious. "What? Why?"

Asher sets the box down on the little table between the two wicker chairs.

"Can't a guy hang out with his little sister every now and then?"

He hands me a cup of coffee, which I take with narrowed eyes. I sip the coffee experimentally. It's actually pretty good.

"Mmm. It depends. I feel like you have ulterior motives." I put the Law Review down.

"Nah, I just have a big box of croissants." He smiles innocently, opening the lid to the box of pastries.

"You are just making me more and more suspicious," I tell him, reaching for a croissant. "I think you should tell me why you're here."

"Just relax," he says, waving a hand at me.

Nothing about Asher has ever made me relaxed. Since we were kids, I have always been running at a full out sprint to catch up to him. Our parents set us up as competitors from the get go.

I realize that, but I'm still put on edge by Asher, just a little bit.

Still, I take him at his word, figuring that whatever he has to tell me must be pretty important. He's showing his hand a little, obfuscating his true intentions too much for it be anything else.

I bite into the croissant, enjoying the flaky and butteriness. "Mmmm."

"Right?" Asher says, smiling. "I got the croissants from Bennett's. They are basically the perfect food."

"Uh huh." I watch him out of the corner of my eye, waiting for him to reveal why he's here. He takes a sip of his coffee, fidgeting.

I have no idea what he's about to say, but I can tell that it's a pretty big deal. He seems to be choosing his words while I sit here, munching on a croissant.

"Hey, do you remember why I made the rule about my friends not being allowed to date you?" he asks.

I arch a brow. "Mmm... not specifically, no."

Asher sits back in his seat, the wicker chair groaning a little beneath him.

"Do you remember Corey Helm?"

I picture Corey immediately. Blonde hair, a weak chin, and overly touchy. "Yeah, unfortunately."

He nods. "Corey was all right, as far as friends go. But he was really weird and creepy around women. He was so desperate, and I think that women just… like, they could tell. They were turned off by it."

"Yeah, he was skeezy." I sip my coffee placidly, wondering what this could possibly have to do with whatever Asher came here to tell me.

"So it wasn't until you had that summer, the one where you sort of… grew up?"

I smile. "You must mean when I was fifteen. The summer that I got boobs?"

He shifts, obviously a little uncomfortable. "Yeah, okay."

I roll my eyes. "And?"

"And we all hung out at our pool all summer, my friends and your group of girls."

"I remember. My friend Karen worshipped you, followed you around like a puppy the whole summer. And you didn't discourage her."

Asher flushes. "That was not one of my more shining moments in time."

I finish my croissant, shrugging. He continues his story.

"Anyway, I remember coming into the pool house. There were a few guys standing there, and Corey was telling them… he was telling them about your… body. In great detail." He pulls a face.

"Ugh, really?" I scrunch up my face. "Gross."

"I totally lost it on him. Not just because no guy should talk about a girl like that. And not just because you're my little sister, although that was part of it."

"No?" I ask, picking at a loose thread on the hem of my tee shirt.

"No. I also lost it because there are almost ten years between you guys! I mean, here you are, so young and like… not ready for that kind of attention from men. And there Corey was, piling it up on top of you anyway."

I squint at my brother for a long second.

"It's nice of you to tell him off for what you saw as inappropriate behavior. It really is. But that's a fact of the world. You can't save me from it just by telling your friends not to harass me."

He looks down. "Yeah, I know. I just— fuck that guy, you know?"

I set my coffee down, patting his shoulder. "I know. Like, fuck the patriarchy too, while we're at it."

He smiles. "Right."

"I have a feeling that you were telling me that story for a reason though, right?"

He nods, taking a sip of his coffee. "Yeah. I was."

"And? Are you going to tell me about you and Evie at some point here?"

Asher looks at me, surprised. "You know already?"

"Of course I know." I sit back, crossing my arms. "You are the most oblivious person ever, I swear."

He winces. "I've been accused of being self-involved before."

"Rightly so, I would say."

He throws up his hands. "All right. I'm the out of touch older brother, then."

I crack a smile. "It's good that you're finally becoming self-aware. I was tiring of how impervious you were to reality."

"You're hilarious, you know that?"

"I try." I pick my coffee up again, considering him. "Is this little admission of yours the opening gambit to something? Are you supposed to be telling me that Evie is moving in with you or something?"

Asher looks a little uncomfortable. "I mean, that's what I want, but she is stubbornly clinging to her independence."

I am impressed, and a little relieved. "Good for her."

"You would be on her side." He sighs. "It's a little more complicated than just me wanting her to move in, though."

"Of course it's complicated," I say. "Nothing that is worthwhile is ever easy."

"Mmm," he says, nodding. "I don't know. Evie has turned my whole world on its axis, it seems like."

I peek inside the pastry box, eyeing a second croissant. "So you just came here to... what, come clean to me about dating her?"

He shrugs. "That's all I've got right now. And actually..." He looks at his phone. "I should probably get going. I have to open Cure a little early today. We have a big liquor shipment coming in this morning."

"Okay." I watch as he stands up, draining his coffee. "I'll take your cup."

"Come by the bar in the next couple of days. I'm trying out a lot of elderflower liquor based cocktails, to appeal to a lighter palate. I'll use you as a guinea pig."

"Okay. See you later."

He heads off the porch, and I sigh. His visit was unexpected, but kind of nice. I may have already known about Asher and Evie, but it was still sort of sweet for him to tell me.

Honestly, it makes me think about Jameson. If my brother had told me this little story a month ago, I probably would have used it as ammunition to ward off any big brotherly fuss about me and Jameson.

Now, of course, it doesn't matter. Jameson made the whole matter moot. But it's still good to know that if A ever puts up any resistance to me dating someone older than me, I can pull the Evie card.

Thinking about Jameson must put some kind of vibrations out there in the universe, because as soon as I settle into reading again, Jameson shows up. He pulls his bike up to the curb outside my house, looking as edible as an ice cream cone. I look at him as he steps off the bike, pulling his helmet off and running a hand through his hair.

He starts towards me, striding up the path in tight denim and a baby blue tee shirt. His dark hair and five o'clock shadow only highlight the intensity in his eyes. My mouth starts to water and my hands begin to shake when I realize that I am the thing that intensity is focused on.

I have to wonder, will there ever be a point when I don't lust after Jameson? When I don't see him and immediately feel like we are the only two people on the planet, like the sun circling the earth? When I don't picture us naked and writhing together, no matter how briefly?

I'm pinned in place by that gaze. I want to strip myself, here and now, and just throw myself at his feet. But of course I don't. I have *some* pride, after all. I just think about it instead.

By the time that he gets to the porch, I've managed to work myself into quite a state. Never mind that I'm supposed to be mad at him for how things ended the other night.

I haven't forgotten that, but it just seems so distant now. Unimportant.

Jameson stops at the porch steps. "I come in peace."

His voice is so rough and gravely, it sends chills down my spine. I cock my head, pretending to consider his words.

"Is that right?" I say. My voice is surprisingly steady, given the gut-churning turmoil that is going on inside my head.

He clears his throat. "Can I come up and sit?"

My mouth feels dry. I incline my head. "Yes."

He climbs the steps. I rake my gaze up the length of his body. I forgot how tall and broad he is, how petite I am in comparison. As he sits down, I bite my lower lip, refusing to admit to myself how much I want him.

I must be hormonal or something, that's for sure. That would explain how my nipples stiffen and my pussy clenches, just looking at him.

Jameson sits down beside me, looking at me with a hesitant expression. "I'm sorry for how things ended the other night. That was not my intention."

I narrow my gaze at him, shifting in place.

"I mean, what else could your intention have been? What did you think was going to happen when you dragged me outside?"

He looks down for a second. "I don't know. I wasn't thinking, obviously. I just... I saw you with that other guy, and I kept thinking... not here. I won't just stand here and watch that guy win Emma over in my space."

I arch a brow. "You realize that is crazy, right? Legitimately nuts."

He scowls. "Yeah, I know. I just... I'm struggling to come to terms with the breakup, okay?"

I sit back, considering him. "Yeah, I am getting that." I purse my lips, thinking. "At least it's not just me that's having a hard time with everything."

Jameson looks up at me, his brown black eyes shining.

"I really am sorry. Will you forgive me?"

I want to reach out and touch him so bad, my fingers itch. Instead, I fold my arms across my chest.

"Yes," I say simply. "But you have to understand that I'm going to move on. Maybe not today, maybe not tomorrow... but eventually. And you can't go around being an asshole about it, either."

Something dark flashes in his eyes, maybe pain. But it's gone before I can put a name to the emotion. It takes him a second to say the words.

"I understand."

I smile a little at him. "Good."

He stands up, shoving his hands into his pockets. "Is there any way that you will still tutor me? Or is that just insanity, thinking that will work?"

I consider that for a second. "I will, if you promise to take me surfing. I want to actually stand up this time."

His face crinkles a bit as he smiles. "I think that's a deal."

"Great." I stand up, even though I haven't got anywhere to go. "Text me?"

"Of course."

Without another word, he lumbers off the porch. I watch him as he heads back to his motorcycle, drawing my lower lip in between my teeth.

11

JAMESON

*L*ying in bed early in the morning, I think of surfing. It is going to be a perfect summer day outside. Blue skies, not a cloud in sight. And the waves are supposed to be killer. I am so burned out with the rest of my life, I can't wait to hit the ocean.

And then I think of Emma. Because I think of her whenever I'm alone in this bed, more often than not stroking my cock and picturing her. I'm not ashamed to admit it, at least to myself.

I miss fucking her.

I imagine Emma, her dark hair streaming down her back, her tits and ass and legs perfectly suntanned against that tiny white bikini of hers. In my mind, she looks over her shoulder and grins at me.

I'm instantly hard, forming a tent under the blankets. I reach down and give my cock a long, lazy stroke, imagining that Emma is sitting on my cock, kissing me. I'd hold onto her thighs to keep her in place, while she would be riding me hard, breathless at the feel of my big cock stretching out her delicate little pussy.

It only takes a minute of imagining her perfect tits bouncing, imagining the sounds that she would make as I fucked her...

I blow my load everywhere, ruining my sheets and comforter as I release with abandon. I stay like that for a minute, then I guiltily get up and gather the sheets and comforter.

This is the third time this week that I've had to wash all my bedding. I blame Emma; it's hard to look at her or think about her without getting crazy fucking blue balls.

As I get dressed to head to the beach, Emma never really leaves my thoughts. Pulling on board shorts and a t-shirt, I think back to the conversation yesterday. She did ask me to text her…

Fuck it. I grab my phone and send her a text, just to see if she's around.

You up?

I'm not expecting anything, but to my surprise she answers almost instantly.

I'm awake. You?

I'm heading to the beach soon. I want to get there by sunrise. You interested?

I wait for a minute, then go about getting my coffee ready. When I check again, there's a response from her.

Will you pick me up?

A grin splits my face. I text her back that I'll be at her place in fifteen minutes, and hurry to get my stuff together. After I find a towel and sunblock, I grab two boards. At the last minute, I fill a thermos with coffee and cream, then I head out to the car.

All the way over to her house in the gray light of morning, I'm in a ridiculously good mood. It's funny how my shitty mood melts away in the face of seeing Emma in a bikini. Part of me thinks that it's sad that I'm so hung up on this girl, but the other part of me is super happy that she's…

Well, she hasn't forgiven me, per se. And nothing has changed. But she's agreed to hang out today, which is about as good as I'm going to get.

I just take those bad feelings and misgivings and stuff them deep down. As I pull up outside Emma's house, I see her front door open.

Then there she is, gorgeous as she has ever fucking been. Her hair is thrown up in a ponytail, she's wearing a jaw-droppingly small electric yellow crop top, and she wears a tantalizing pair of ridiculously tiny black shorts.

She jogs up to my Jeep, wrenching the door open and piling herself inside. She has a backpack too, probably to hold her wetsuit. She looks at me, a small smile on her lips.

"Hi," she says.

"Hi yourself," I say mildly, throwing the car into drive.

"Can we drive through somewhere to get coffee?" she asks, yawning a little. I wait as she puts on her seatbelt, trying not to let my gaze linger for too long on those sun kissed bare legs. "It's soooo early."

"I've already got some, if you don't mind sharing," I say, jerking my thumb toward the back seat. "It's in the thermos."

"You think I'm going to turn down free coffee?" She fishes the thermos out of the backseat. When she unscrews the lid, the smell of dark roast permeates the air for a second. "Even if it does mean catching your cooties."

I give her a look, teasing her right back. "Hey, you don't have to drink it."

She pours a little in the cap, then sips it. "Coffee is coffee."

"I'll have to remember that." I pull up to the beachside parking area at the beach just as the sunrise really makes itself known. The beach looks amazing like this, the light reaching out warm fingers to touch a cold wave here, a dune of sand there.

"Wow, there's like... no one here," Emma marvels, gawking at the empty beach. And she's right, there are only a couple of cars parked here this early.

I park the Jeep. "Getting up this early for anything is pretty foreign to a lot of people."

"I see that. I mean, I'm usually one of those people." She smiles as she recaps the thermos and climbs out of the car.

I avert my gaze again instead of staring at her ass, which I guarantee looks fantastic when she's bent over in those shorts. I don't need to be walking around with a big ass boner while we're just carrying stuff from the Jeep onto the beach. I don't want her to think I'm a total pervert.

Although, I am. And she knows that I am.

I groan as I pick up the boards and my backpack, heading straight down into the sand. Emma follows, shouldering her own little backpack. I pick a spot pretty close to where the surf comes running onto the beach, figuring with the waning tide that our stuff should be safe enough from the water there.

"Here okay?" I say, looking at Emma.

She drops her backpack, which I take as a sign that she's satisfied with the spot.

"Looks good to me," she says, shading her eyes against the rising sun. "I'm really hoping that I can stand up this time."

"You can, for sure," I say, dropping the boards. I unzip my backpack, pulling the sunblock and my wetsuit out. "You feel like sharing some of that coffee?"

She gives me a lopsided grin. "Yep."

Emma pours a little bit of coffee into the thermos cap, and passes it over. I slurp the coffee down, trying not to stare as she takes off her tiny top and shorts. I set the thermos cap atop the boards as she wiggles her beautiful body inside her wetsuit.

Looking down at the sand, I strip off my t-shirt and pull off my shoes, then work my way into my wetsuit. I only pull my wetsuit halfway on, leaving my torso bare.

When I look up, I catch Emma watching me, her gaze heavy and heated. She blushes when she sees me notice her looking.

There's an awkward moment where I'm grinning and she's trying not to smile.

"We're both still hot, in case you hadn't noticed," I say, trying to relieve the tension.

She arches a brow. "Is that so?"

"Yep. Just because we aren't actively fucking doesn't make it any different."

I try to keep my tone light and casual. Inside, I'm dying to know whether she still wants me as badly as I want to be with her. She just blushes and shakes her head at me.

"That's good to know." Her smile is tight-lipped, suggesting that maybe I shouldn't drag old feelings out into the sunlight.

"Are you ready to go straight for it, or do you maybe want a refresher?"

Emma seems indecisive. "Uhhh… maybe you should just remind me what the steps are? Like, verbally, I mean."

"Okay. Starting from the end of the board, yeah?" I point to the end of one of the surf boards. "You grab the sides, and then move onto your stomach. Then you lift yourself upward…"

"Oh, right. Then I sort of turn my leg…"

"Yep. And slide your other foot forward. Then the hard part, which is having enough balance to stand and surf."

"Right. Got it." She scrunches her face up. "I mean, I think I do."

"Good. Let's paddle out, then."

I pick up the thermos lid, putting it back on top of the thermos. Then I hand one of the surf boards to her. We pad out to the sea, the sand stiff and crunchy, breaking away under our feet. When I step into the ocean and feel it swirl around my feet, I suck in a deep lungful of salty air.

Glancing at Emma to make sure she's still with me, I put my surfboard down on the water.

"Don't forget to attach your leash to your ankle," I say. Balancing awkwardly for a second, I put the leash on my ankle.

I look at her as she does the same, biting her lip as she attaches the leash. I can't help the way my eyes dip down to her lush mouth, or the way they slide down to her tits. Most of her body is covered in the wetsuit, but I notice that the zipper is only pulled up to her breasts, leaving plenty of room for the imagination to lurk in the sweet shadows found there.

I realize that I am as bad as a horny fucking teenager, filling in what I can't see. But I don't bother to jerk my gaze away this time.

She looks up and colors when she sees me looking at her. She tucks a strand of hair behind her ear. "What?"

I grin. "Nothing. Are you ready to try to surf?"

She starts to move out away from the shore. "Yeah, I—" Then her face suddenly contorts. "OWWW!"

She pulls away from where she just stepped and leans her weight on her left leg, her expression agonized.

"Whoa, are you okay?" I ask, looking around. I look into the water around her, but it's murky, lots of sand swirling around her body.

Emma is actually in tears. "I think I got stung by a jellyfish. It really *hurts*!"

"Okay, let's go back to the shore. Can you walk?"

She shakes her head, her face burning. When she speaks, her voice is choked with tears. "I don't think so."

"Come here," I say, crouching and scooping her up in my arms. She weighs nothing, her small body wracked with sobs. Her hands settle around my shoulders, clinging to me as she tries to control her crying. I head to the shore, murmuring soothing things to her. "It's okay. You're okay."

I'm slowed down by the fact that I'm dragging two surf boards, but I eventually make it out of the water with Emma in my arms. As soon as we're clear of the water, I slip my leash off and unfasten hers too.

Leaving the boards behind us, I carry her to the spot where we left our stuff. I go down onto my knees instead of dropping her, placing her gently on the sand.

She immediately starts trying to look at her right foot, while I dig in my bag for the first aid kit I keep in there. I pull out the little bottle of vinegar that I keep on hand for just such an occasion.

"Let me see." I move us both so that her foot is in my lap, examining it with a tender touch. I see the jellyfish sting, a perfectly clear line of welts that practically glow bright red. "I think you were actually pretty lucky, it doesn't look like there are any tentacles to remove or anything."

"Oww!" she yelps when I move her foot a little too suddenly.

"I'm sorry," I say, uncapping the vinegar. "This is probably going to sting a little bit at first."

Emma nods her head, biting her lip. Tears roll down her face as I pour the vinegar on her sting. She winces, but doesn't react otherwise.

After about half a minute, she lets out a big breath. "It's not as bad anymore. Omigod, it was so bad."

I rub her leg for a second. "I bet."

She looks up, wiping away the remnants of her tears. Our gazes connect, and for the longest moment, I'm a little lost in the green mystery of her eyes.

After a minute, she glances down. "I don't think I'm surfing today, Jameson."

"Nope. We'll try again, though." I smile encouragingly at her.

Her lips lift in the ghost of a smile. "Okay. Sounds good."

I lift her foot off of my lap and start to get our stuff together.

12

JAMESON

I stretch, checking my phone. It's almost five and I'm sitting on a couch in a coffee shop, waiting for Emma to turn up. She's only about ten minutes late, which is par for the course with her. I glance around at the shop, which is mostly empty.

"Sir?" a young woman asks, catching me by surprise. She's the same woman that made my latte when I first got here, over an hour ago. "We're actually going to close a little early, if you don't mind."

"Sure, yeah." I get up, grabbing my backpack and my empty latte cup.

"I'll take that," she says, whisking the cup out of my hands. "Have a nice day!"

I nod, heading out of the shop. I have to give it to the barista, I've never been told to fuck off in such a nice way before.

As I step outside into the breezy summer afternoon, Emma comes rushing up to me. She is wearing a slinky little white sundress, baring a good amount of cleavage and leg, which to me makes up for her lateness.

"Sorry I'm late!!" she apologizes. "I swear, I left my house at a reasonable time…"

"It doesn't really matter. The coffee shop is closing early, so we're free agents now."

"Really?" Emma peers in the coffee shop's window, as if I might be wrong.

I shade my eyes. "Yeah. Listen, I'm starving. Are you hungry enough to eat?"

"Uhhh..." She seems indecisive. "Aren't we going to study?"

"Totally. I just thought since we are right here, we might as well go to Casa Carne, because it's just across the street. They have the best fucking tacos, I swear."

She flips back her long dark hair. "Yeah, I guess that's okay."

"Come on. I feel like you probably haven't even had any real food today." I look both ways before I start to cross the street. "Right?"

She goes pink, rushing to follow me. "Maybe."

Once we're across the street, I slow down, out of respect for the fact that she is so much shorter than me. I look for the festive red green and white flag, which is the only thing that denotes that the taco truck even exists.

"Is this it?" she asks, wrinkling her nose.

"Don't make that face," I tell her, sidling up to the cart's open window.

"The menu is all in Spanish!" she protests.

"Trust me, okay? I'll order for you. You don't eat chicken, beef, or pork, right?"

She gives me a long look, then slowly nods. "Yeah..."

"Hola," I say, greeting the middle aged guy who runs the cart. "Que pasa?"

"De nada," the guy says, his voice surprisingly deep. "What will you have?"

"Let me get the chilaquiles, two barbacoa tacos, and two tinga tacos. A tofu taco for her... and two of the vegetarian pupusas. Oh, and let me also get two Cokes." I glance behind me, and see a little patio setup that is currently empty. "For here, please."

"You got it. That's gonna be... twenty two dollars."

We exchange currency, with me leaving a fat tip in the tip bucket. He hands me the Cokes, after he uncaps the bottles. He starts cooking, and I point to the two little tables.

"Your choice," I tell her.

She chooses one of the tables, and I sit down in a plastic chair across from her. I pass her Coke over, and she takes a long sip. She settles down, considering me.

"You come here often?"

I slide my backpack to the floor. "Not often enough. I love the food though. It's the food that I almost spent my life making."

"Wait, what?"

"Yeah. I had two job opportunities at the same time. One was bar-backing at a dive bar. The other was working at a place just like this. I often wonder what would've happened if I hadn't chosen the job I did."

Emma considers that for a minute. "I feel like you would've been successful no matter what industry you chose. You just bring a certain passion to any job, and customers can tell. That's what makes you succeed."

I frown. "I don't know about all of that."

She rolls her eyes. "Take it from me, okay? I'm telling you. You're smart, and you're a go-getter."

I clear my throat a little. "I mean, I'm only doing well because your brother thought he should invest in the business."

"My brother was the lucky one, Jameson. If he didn't invest in you, someone else would have, for sure. The reason that Asher has good business sense is because he is smart enough to see as opportunity when it's right in front of his dumb face."

She takes another long pull on the Coke, her throat working delicately. As she crosses her long legs, I tamp down any reaction I feel, either about her looking so good or about her compliments.

Instead, I change the subject.

"Do you ever think, if I hadn't gone to law school, what would I do?" I ask.

At that moment, the food cart guy comes over, his arms loaded down with plates. "Hot food, okay?"

"Thanks," I say, my mouth watering when I get a whiff of the barbacoa beef and chicken tinga.

"Omigod, look at all of this!" Emma exclaims. "It looks amazing."

I set us each up a plate, dividing the tacos and the pupusas. The chilaquiles I put between us, letting the mixture of eggs, peppers and onions, and tortilla strips cool down to earthly temperatures.

She takes a bite of the tinga taco, and then moans loudly. "This is so good!!"

I take a bite of my pupusa, savoring the corn tortilla and the cheesy filling. She's right, it's just as phenomenal as I thought it would be.

We eat for a minute, our mouths too full to bother with words.

"You didn't answer my question from before," I point out, sipping my Coke. "What would you be if you weren't a lawyer in training?"

"Mmm! I don't know." She wrinkles her nose. "I feel like I was set on this path from a young age. I had the option of being a lawyer, or a housewife. And fuck being a housewife, you know?"

She takes a forkful of the chilaquiles, mmming her appreciation.

"Alright, but if you could be anything at all. You could design rockets or make clothes or… anything. What would you be?"

She takes a huge bite of her tofu taco, and takes a minute to chew. "Hmmm. I think I'd be a veterinarian, maybe? I really love animals a lot."

That surprises me. "Yeah? I've never seen you own a pet, I don't think."

She wags a finger at me. "That's because I don't mess with small animals. No, I'd be a large animal vet. Horses, cows... maybe bison and deer."

"Really? Man, I can't see you doing that."

She chuckles. "Yeah, well. I love riding horses. I did dressage all through school. Even into college, as a matter of fact."

"What the fuck is dressage?" I ask, imagining something that involves dresses.

"It's horseback riding. You know, English saddles, women wearing knee-length leather boots. Horses with their manes braided. All that jazz."

I just grunt, looking at her. I can see it though. A girl with her background riding horses makes a lot of sense to me.

"Don't give me that look," she accuses me. "Every single girl in my class did dressage."

I just eat my pupusa and keep my thoughts to myself.

"Hey, do you remember the Halloween that you and Asher took me and my friends trick or treating?" Emma asks, pushing her mostly finished plate away.

"Of course I remember," I say. "You were a fancy lady, if I recall."

Her dimples flash. "I was the historical figure of Elizabeth Cady Stanton, one of the first leaders of the women's rights movement."

I shake my head, balling up a napkin and tossing it on my plate. "You'll have to go easy on me. Remember, I dropped out of school. I'm fucking dumb, and I always will be."

I expect her to roll her eyes, but she doesn't. Instead, she grows solemn for a minute.

"You are not dumb. Seriously, you're so smart. I wasn't kidding earlier when I said you would be successful no matter what you did."

I roll my eyes, my face heating. "Don't say that."

"What? Why not?"

"Because I know that you're doing it to be nice, but it's still a bunch of bullshit."

She seems taken aback by that. "No, it's not. I'm being completely honest. You might have dropped out, but I've seen your bookshelf at your house. Shakespeare, Herman Melville, David Foster Wallace... that is not what a stupid person reads, okay?"

I just wave her away. I know what's true and what's false, and the line she keeps repeating about my intelligence is just not true. "Alright. Whatever. Let's talk about something else."

Emma sighs. "Okay. What do you want to talk about, then?"

"Uhhh..." I wrack my brain for something else to talk about. I finally come up with something, but when I say it aloud, it sounds super lame. "How are your parents?"

There's a palpable tension in the air. Not so much between me and Emma, but between her and her parents. I notice that she straightens her spine a little and clears her throat.

"They're fine. They are... they're trying to encourage me to date people that they approve of." She looks down, fidgeting with the hem of her sundress.

"Oh." I'm not sure how to respond to that. "Any luck so far?"

I watch her expressive face grow quietly sad. It's painful to watch. Painful to be part of a conversation where she talks about dating people who aren't me.

I know that I should be the only one she thinks of. She knows it too.

But to preserve our fragile truce, neither of us says it.

She keeps her eyes on the hem of her dress. "Not really. There are a few guys that my mother thinks will be a good match, whatever that means."

"That's... good." I honestly can't think of anything else to say.

"What about you?" she asks, looking up at me.

"What do you mean?"

"I mean like... you know. Who are you dating?"

Something like hope shimmers in those emerald green eyes of hers.

"No one." I shift in my seat, beyond uncomfortable with this line of questioning. What I want to say, what I should say, is *there will never be anyone else for me but you.*

But I don't. She bites her bottom lip.

"I see."

I really doubt that she does, but I'm eager to let it go.

"Are you ready to go find somewhere to study?" I ask, getting to my feet. I start to gather the paper plates on the table.

"Sure," she says. I glance at her, and I can see that something is weighing on her. But I don't want to talk about any of it anymore.

So I throw the paper plates out and thank the food cart dude. Then I lead Emma back out onto the street.

13

EMMA

I'm on the street in front of the pizza place that Jameson took me to, chewing on a nail. I don't want to be here. I especially don't like the fact that I am dressed up — wearing a skimpy black body con dress, no less.

But my mother nagged me about going out with Rich enough times that I finally threw my hands up and agreed. I know that it is a bad idea, but I do it anyway.

Anything to please the family, right?

I'm not certain about any of that now, as I am standing here sweating my ass off while I wait for Rich to show. He's almost fifteen minutes late, and I am seriously about to call an Uber.

If he can't be bothered to be on time for our first date, it doesn't bode well for the future.

"Emma?"

I turn to find Jameson and Forest walking up. I can feel Jameson's eyes all over me in such a conspicuous outfit... of course, with him it feels sort of naughty.

"Hi?" I say, brushing back a lock of hair. "I didn't expect to see you two today."

"David invited us," Forest says. "You look nice, by the way."

I flush. "Oh, thanks. I'm, um... I'm on a date."

Jameson's expression turns dark as a thundercloud. "Here?"

I bite my lip, glancing over my shoulder. It takes a deep breath before I can answer. I try to smile, turning on the charm.

"Yeah. I mean, he's late, but whenever he gets here."

Jameson just glowers at me, which makes me feel like total trash. I couldn't have known that he would be here today, though.

"We should go inside," Forest says, pulling Jameson by the arm. "It was nice seeing you, Emma."

Jameson lets Forest lead him on toward the front door of the restaurant, but he glances back to me. He doesn't say anything, but his eyes speak volumes.

How could you do this? and *This isn't what I wanted* are chief among them. It chills me to the bone. I know that I had no choice but to move on from him, but it still feels like shit.

So I glance down, breaking the connection. I can't do anything else.

I pull out my phone, trying to decide between calling an Uber and going home or just changing the restaurant. I can't go inside, obviously. But Rich is almost twenty minutes late at this point... is there any way I can just call it?

Uncertain, I suck in another deep breath.

"Emma!"

I glance up to see Rich, dressed in sweaty workout clothes. I give him a puzzled look. I definitely said that we were going to dinner at a nice place.

"You look fancy," he says. He closes in, apparently going for a hug.

"This dress is Valentino," I grit out, backing away from his embrace. "And I told you that we were going somewhere nice for dinner!"

"You said it was pizza," he says, defensive.

"No, I definitely said a fancy Italian restaurant. I explicitly told you to wear something nice." I'm miffed that he is even bothering to argue with me.

Rich looks down at his sweaty, rumpled clothes and shrugs. "I'm sure they'll take us."

The wind shifts, and I get a whiff of him. I wrinkle my nose; he doesn't just smell sweaty, he reeks, like he hasn't *ever* showered. How did I not notice that at my parents' party?

"Yeah, we can't go in there," I say, motioning to the restaurant behind me. "It's well into dinner time. We missed our reservation, and besides, they definitely have a dress code for dinner."

"Psssh," he says, waving a hand. "I just have to grease a palm or two. Trust me, it's nothing I haven't done a hundred times."

He doesn't even realize how entitled he sounds. It really steams me. "Rich—"

"Uh uh," he says, grasping my arm and whipping me around. I'm so shocked by it, my mouth falls open. "Methinks she doth protest too much, right? Come on, you wanted to go here, so we'll go here."

His grip on my arm is like iron. I stumble forward to the door of the restaurant, unable to put the words together to tell him off.

We get inside the bustling little place, and I see that it is jam packed. A young man comes up to the host stand.

"Hi. Do you have a reservation?" he asks.

"We do. Right, babe?" Rich says, looking to me.

I try not to make an ugly face. "We had one at seven thirty under Alderisi."

The host gives us a disapproving look, and begins typing my name into an iPad he has at the host stand. I get another whiff of Rich's body odor, and I almost vomit.

The host surveys Rich. "I'm sorry, but while I do have your reservation still, I don't believe that you meet our dress code."

Rich lets go of my arm and reaches in his pocket, producing several bills. He peels off two, slapping them down on the host stand.

"There!" he declares. "Just to let you know that I'm serious about dropping some dough in this place." He laughs. "See what I did there? Dropping some dough? Because this is a pizza place?"

Though I would like him not to take Rich's money, the host discreetly pockets the bills. "If you want to come right this way, I'll show you to your table."

Rolling my eyes, I follow the host through the restaurant... Right to the table behind Jameson and Forest. Jameson sees me, glowers, and then spots Rich. His expression turns puzzled as he looks back and forth between Rich and me. Like he's trying to piece us together, but keeps coming up lacking.

The host seats us, and Rich takes the seat facing away from Jameson and Forest. He plunks down without a second thought, and I'm left to sit with Jameson in plain view. I feel my cheeks heating as I sit.

Could this date get much worse? If it can, I don't want to know.

Rich picks up the drinks menu. "You like cocktails?"

I put my purse on my chair, lining my gaze up so that Rich is blocking Jameson. I pick up the food menu. "I don't know. Sort of?"

Rich grabs the first server that walks by. "Hey! We'll have a couple of tequila sunrises, right here."

My brows knit. "I don't drink tequila."

"You'll love it," he says, picking up the food menu. "Oooh, they have a ribeye. That's what I'm going to get. You should maybe get a salad or something."

My mouth opens, but once again he has robbed me of words. Everything he's saying and doing is classic bad date behavior. It's almost like he is testing me, trying to see what I'll tolerate.

"I don't think so," I say, narrowing my eyes at Rich. "I think I'm going to get the funghi pizza."

He doesn't so much as put his menu down. He just talks to me over it, which is beyond rude. "All right. Just don't complain to me when you've gained weight, okay? I know how you women are."

His words are so outrageous, I can't even take him seriously.

I lean over just a bit, beyond Rich, and find Jameson still watching. He sees me looking, and raises his eyebrows.

I lean back, embarrassed that I was caught out so clearly.

The waiter brings our drinks and takes our orders. I taste the drink he put before me, but I'm immediately overwhelmed with the taste of tequila.

"Blech," I say, pushing the drink away.

Rich just shrugs and downs his drink right away, then reaches for mine. "Don't mind if I do."

Rich proceeds to get drunk very quickly. He also grows more aggressive and more sexual with every drink.

"So what I'm saying is, basically, that if a woman doesn't suck my dick, why even keep her around?" Rich says, draining his sixth drink. "You get it, right?"

At this point, I'm so repulsed by him, it's not even funny. To have this privileged guy who smells like the worst of the gym socks telling me how he expects to get head regularly from the girls he sees? I don't even know how he functions in day to day life. Money only goes so far to protect you.

I push my chair back, standing up. "I think we can just cut the date off here. I think it's clear that we don't belong together."

"What? No, come on," he says, drunkenly getting to his feet. "The food hasn't even come yet. Lemme find a waiter."

He turns to look for someone, but I just give Rich a tight smile. "I don't think that we need the food to be able to tell that we're not suited. I'm going to go."

I step out from the table, scooting my chair in. I intend to leave with a little dignity, and block Rich's phone number in my phone as soon as my Uber gets here.

"Don't," Rich says, his voice a growl.

I turn and hurry between the rows of tables, rushing out the door of the restaurant.

"You had better stop!" Rich yells, his footfalls indicating that he's right on my heels.

He catches me just outside the front door, grabbing my arms and hauling me up against the rough stucco of the building. He's sweating. When he speaks, his words are flecked with foam.

"Where the *fuck* do you think you're going?"

He slams me against the building hard enough to make my head crack against the stucco. I gasp, seeing stars.

"Nobody leaves me, especially not a damaged little rich girl like you. Your father had to beg me to even take you out, you *slut*." He slams me against the wall again.

Out of the corner of my eye, I see the door open. Jameson steps out, takes one look at what's going on, and completely loses his shit.

"Get the fuck off her!" Jameson howls, tackling Rich from the side. "Motherfucker—"

"Fuck you!" Rich says, falling over. He pulls Jameson down and tries to punch him. He only manages to land one blow, but it's a pretty good one, damaging Jameson's nose.

Jameson starts to bleed really heavily. That seems to make Jameson really mad.

"I'll fucking end you," Jameson promises, something triggered in him.

He starts whaling on Rich, his fists hitting the guy's face with a series of muffled thuds. The two men are locked together, grunting and cursing. Rich struggles to fight back a little.

"Jameson, no!" I cry out, helpless. People begin to file out of the restaurant, and Forest tries to get between them. He fails, though.

Across the street, a police cruiser turns the corner, sees the people crowded around the fight, and turns on its lights. Forest comes over to me, grabbing me and pushing himself between me and the crowd. In a few seconds, the cops are jumping out of the car, pulling Jameson off of Rich.

"Wait, officer, it wasn't his fault!" I yell when one of the cops hauls Jameson up off the ground and slams him against the patrol car. The other officer is doing the same thing to Rich.

I am suddenly aware that I am crying, and I feel deeply ashamed.

"Ma'am, please get back," the officer says to me. "All of you need to get back, right now."

Forest pulls me away, watching the cop's every movement like a hawk. "It's okay," he murmurs to me, but I can tell that he doesn't mean it.

"Please, no—" I try again to intervene, but the cops are already cuffing and searching both of the men. Forest wraps his arms around me and carries me back a few feet.

Jameson makes eye contact with me, and I dissolve into a mess of tears in Forest's arms. As Jameson is put into the back of the patrol car, I turn in Forest's arms, crying into his neck.

14

JAMESON

I'm lying down on a cot in the jail cell the cops stuck me in, staring at the ceiling. It's stiflingly hot in this cell, and the walls are just plain cinder blocks. I've been here for six hours, long enough for the cops to have booked me into the system. My fingertips are still black with the now-dry ink.

I haven't been in here long enough to be wearing anything other than my blood stained shirt and jeans, though. I reflexively touch my face, thinking of the source of most of the blood.

My nose is swollen, sensitive to my touch. I try to ignore that. It's not hard, because I keep replaying in my mind what happened.

I open the door of the restaurant. I look to my right, and there is pretty little Emma, being slammed up against the building by that douchebag.

Then I lose control.

I rewind it in my head a little, coming back again and again to look at one particular thing. The terrified look in Emma's eyes, the way he had his hands on her arms, his fingers digging into her flesh…

No one touches Emma like that, ever. I would be upset over

any woman getting hurt in front of me, but that stupid idiot touched her. A girl that a part of me still thought of as *mine*.

It's no surprise that I saw red.

There was no doubt in my mind, then or now, that I did the right thing. As soon as the cops rolled up, I shut my mouth, refusing to say anything. I have heard stories about people that talk without a lawyer present, and they're not pretty. So I asked for a lawyer as soon as I was arrested, and the police haven't pushed me on that yet.

I'll be damned if I'm going to wind up in court for defending a woman from an abuser. So I've been biding my time, trying not to get too worked up over the fact that I am trapped in this brick room with absolutely no view outside.

I adjust the flimsy pillow that's under my head. With no phone and nothing else to distract me, I find myself focusing on Emma. Replaying the whole night, again and again, almost like meditating.

Seeing her enter the restaurant with that ridiculous man child. Feeling my chest tighten every time she leaned over and glanced at me around Forest's head. Watching as she fled the restaurant.

Flinging the front door open to find her pinned against the wall, helpless and afraid.

If I could go back in time and do it all again, I would do it the same damn way. Even though it landed me here, I would rather be in here and know that my girl is safe.

My girl. My mouth twists at that. All I can say right now is fuck Asher for making that stupid rule, and fuck me too for following it.

"Jameson Hart!" a guard shouts outside my cell. I sit up, tensing. The door unlocks, and the guard swings it open, looking in. "You're free to go. Come on."

Not one to question being given my freedom, I spring up. I follow the guard down a labyrinth of hallways, stopping at a window to collect my shoes, my phone, and my wallet.

"Am I being charged with anything?" I ask the guard as I put my shoes back on.

"Nah. Richard Spencer, the guy you pounded? He basically wouldn't stop talking once he got here. He admitted to throwing the first punch, and to assaulting the girl he was with. What a fuckin' piece of work. I'm glad you gave him what he was askin' for."

The guard rolls his eyes and shakes his head.

I just nod, figuring that I'll stick to not talking to the cops, regardless of the circumstances. It takes a few more minutes for them to go through my release paperwork. I keep my trap shut and sign where they tell me.

The next thing I know, I'm stepping out into the humid night air. I look around at the nondescript parking lot that I exited to, checking my phone. I have a whole bunch of texts and missed calls from Forest and Asher, telling me to call them if and when I get out.

I don't feel like calling one of them for a ride though, honestly. I just want to take a shower and lay in my own bed. I open the Uber app and search for a ride home.

"Jameson?"

I look up to find Emma heading my way after sliding out of a strange black Range Rover, looking tired as hell. She has to walk a fair distance from her car to where I'm standing; I start to walk towards her, a little dazed that she would even be here.

She went home and changed, obviously, because she's wearing a plain black t-shirt and a little denim skirt. But her hair is a mess, and she's wearing fluffy bunny slippers on her feet.

She has never looked so good to me as she does now, barreling towards me in the parking lot.

"Hey—" I start to greet her. Then I groan as she all but tackles me, hugging me around the torso so hard that I wince.

I stand there for a second, stunned. Of all the reactions that I expected, this wasn't one of them. I wrap my arms around her, enjoying the feel of her in my arms.

Emma looks up at me, tears shining in her eyes. "Thank you for coming to my defense, Jameson. I am so, so sorry that you got arrested because of me."

She hugs me again, slipping her arms around my neck and burying her face against my neck. I can't resist the urge to lean down and smell her hair, taking a deep inhalation of her feminine scent.

"You weren't to blame," I murmur against her hair, cradling her head. "You did nothing wrong."

She doesn't even look at me this time. "I went on a date with him, didn't I?"

"You can't have known it would end up like this." I gently pry her back a couple of inches, even though I never want to let her go. Her tear stained face breaks my heart. "I can't stand to see you cry."

Her emerald eyes are large and mesmerizing, her face sweetly heart shaped. I cup the side of her face in one hand, pushing back some of her wild hair. Her lips are luscious and inviting, and they part ever so slightly when my gaze drops to look at them.

I don't honestly know whether I move first or she does, but we both surge forward. My lips find hers, hesitating at first. But once I get the taste of her in my mouth, the scent of her in my nose, I go wild.

Then there is nothing gentle about the way that I grab her, hauling her up against me. I'm already hard for her, imagining the sweet satisfaction that I'm about to find at the apex of her thighs. My tongue seeks hers and she opens her mouth to me, urging me on.

Emma makes this sound, a mewling sound, but more guttural. The sound makes the fine hair on the back of my neck stand up and my whole body tingles for a second. I pull her body up against mine, rubbing her tits across my chest. She moans and wraps her legs around my torso.

Fuck, she feels so good. Far better than in my imagination. I carry her back towards her car, trying to figure out how I'm going to get her back to my house. It seems impossible to put her down and calmly drive somewhere else, but I can't just have sex with her here in the parking lot of the jail, either.

She starts to kiss my neck, sucking hard on my earlobe. My eyes roll into the back of my head for the briefest moment and I stumble. Emma seems totally unworried about our surroundings.

Maybe she's completely oblivious to my thought process about how I can fuck her the fastest. But when I get to her car, pressing her against the driver's side door, she looks up at me. Her eyes are filled with the same impatient lust as mine.

"Take me right here, right now," she demands, her voice low and throaty. "I need you, Jameson."

Lust fills my veins like lead. Her words are the balm I've needed for so long; it feels like it's been aeons since I've been inside her, instead of weeks.

Still, I shake my head. "No. Not here."

"Yes," she whispers in my ear. She grabs my hand, pulling it down her body, until I'm touching the front of her panties. They're damp, soaked by her need. Her words turn pleading. "Now. In the car. I need you inside me right now."

At the same time, she reaches down between us, feeling the outline of my cock through my pants.

Fuck. It's hard to think, hard to speak. Especially when she pleads so sweetly for me to fuck her.

Emma pulls the keys for the Range Rover and unlocks the car. She puts her feet down and wriggles a little bit to try to pull on the door handle.

"Uh uh," I say, my eyes burning into hers. I step back, leaving her looking at me with a note of shock on her face. She thinks I'm turning down sex, which is almost funny. "If you need it as badly as you say, get your ass in the back and fold the seats down. I need room to work."

Her eyes widen a bit, but she hurries around to the very back of the car, opening the gate. I don't give her any space or time. I'm right on her heels, watching her as she puts the seats down.

As soon as she makes the back seat flat, I give her a little push. "Get inside," I order.

I get immense pleasure out of watching her miles of fantastic legs and ass as she scurries into the back of the Range Rover. I climb in the back, pulling down the gate behind me.

It's still a little crowded, being that I'm almost six and a half feet tall. But when she gets herself turned around, biting her lip and looking up at me, I suddenly feel that same urgency as I felt earlier.

And when Emma starts to undress, pulling her shirt up over her head, that urgency takes over. I pull my shirt off too, lying down.

"Get your panties off," I growl. "I want you to ride me, right fucking now."

She looks at me with those wide, innocent eyes and starts to unzip her skirt.

"No. Leave it on," I tell her. "And take the panties off. Don't make me tell you again."

I unzip my own pants as she shimmies her panties down her legs, kicking them off with her shoes. I hook my thumbs into the waistband of my boxer briefs, shoving them and my pants down to the middle of my thighs.

My cock springs free, long and thick, the tip of it already slick with precum. Emma's hand is on my cock instantly, her fist closing around it.

Fuck, that feels so good.

It's been so long since I felt her little fist gripping my dick that I close my eyes when she touches me. She gives me a few experimental strokes, testing the waters. But when I see her head going down to my cock, I have to stop her.

"No, not now," I grit out, guiding her face up to mine. "I don't want to blow my load in your mouth. I want your pussy, and I want it right now."

She straddles me, breathing a little bit faster. I force her head down and kiss her, even as I lift my hips up. My cock touches her warm inner thigh. I close my eyes for the briefest moment, distracting myself with the names of gin brands.

Genever, Bombay, Tanqueray, Beefeater, Citadelle, Aviation, Hendrick's, Seagrams...

I open my eyes, realizing that I should've definitely jacked off in the last couple days. Or maybe been with a girl that was less hot than Emma, who was straight up bombshell.

I kiss her, pressing her ass down so that her knees widen.

"You're going to have to ride slow," I warn. "I'm so fucking hot for you right now, I can barely see straight."

She gives me a wicked grin. "Is that right?"

I just grunt, pressing her down again. I use my free hand to stand my cock straight up, groaning when the blunt tip touches her pussy lips. They are already dripping with moisture.

Emma's been waiting for me, it seems.

She sinks down on my dick, her expression enraptured. I have to close my eyes and list whiskey brands while she stretches to take all of me.

"Fuck!" I mutter. "God damn, you're so tight, baby. So wet. So perfect."

When she finally takes all of my cock, I pull her down for a long, slow kiss.

"Are you ready?" she asks, already breathless.

To answer her question, I move my hips upward. She cries out, but she doesn't stop. No, she keeps going, her actions growing frenzied. Her pussy grips my cock as she rides me.

I move my hand down between our bodies, rubbing her clit. I am going to make damn sure that she comes when I do... and I'm going to come pretty damn soon.

"Oh my god," she says, leaning forward. "Omigod, right there..."

I can feel her tensing and clenching, getting close to the edge.

"Fuck. That's right. I love the way you ride me, Em. The way that sweet pussy grips my cock so tight—"

That little bit of dirty talk is enough to push her over the edge. She cries out, her pussy spasming wildly, her nails scoring the flesh of my chest.

I let myself go, pumping up into her body with abandon. I can feel the orgasm before it hits, feel it down low in my balls. It tears loose and I thrust upward again and again, her greedy little pussy milking my cock of every drop.

I slow, then stop, trying to catch my breath. She lays sprawled across my chest, her breathing rapid, covered in a layer of sweat. Not just hers, but mine, too.

I close my eyes and hold her close, enjoying the musky smells coming from us both, and the moment of closeness.

It's not enough, just being with her. It's not nearly enough.

But I'll take what I can get, for right now.

15

EMMA

Afterward, Jameson drives my Range Rover back to my house. He doesn't stop touching me the whole way, his right hand traveling from my bare knee to my outer thigh and back down. I lean into the contact, my arm entwined with his. I stroke his muscular biceps through his shirt, biding my time until I can get him naked again.

He looks at me more than he should while he drives, his gaze possessive. And he keeps stroking my knee and my thigh, his fingertips scrawling lazily across my skin. It's as if he's been so starved for touch that he can't help himself; I know that's the way I feel, at least.

No words pass between us as he drives. There are no questions about what we're doing, no angry denials of feelings. None of that.

I assume that he feels the same way that I do. I don't know a hundred percent, but I expect that he isn't sure why we were ever not together.

Maybe later, we'll talk about that. But not now.

When we get to my house, he is as eager to get inside as I am. We kiss and embrace on the porch as I hunt down my key. I put the key in the lock, and he runs his tongue along the shell of my ear.

"Someone will see us," I warn him, gasping as he reaches around to cup my breasts.

"So?"

I turn the key and push the door open, a shiver running down my spine at his response. Is he really so cavalier about it now?

I swallow the question, because now isn't the time for all of that. There will be infinite amounts of time to discuss it later. I turn in his arms, kissing him. He grabs me and lifts me up, carrying me inside.

I squeak a little as he kicks the door shut. He carries me straight into my bedroom, collapsing on the bed on top of me. We take our time, kissing and exploring. He goes down on me and makes me cum three times before he is ready for sex.

And unsurprisingly, Jameson makes me cum again while he's deep inside me. When we're finished, both laying exhaustedly together, he kisses me so slowly and throughly that my eyes mist over.

I bury my head against his neck to hide my tears, but he's having none of it.

"Hey," Jameson says softly. He lifts my chin with gentle fingers. "You're crying again."

"I know," I sniff, embarrassed. "Sorry, it's just… overwhelming."

"There's nothing to apologize for." His arm tightens around my shoulders, holding me a little closer.

A minute of silence passes between us. I'm wondering where I should begin to broach the topic of the huge change we just made to our relationship. While I'm thinking, though, Jameson speaks.

"I should be the one to apologize," he says after a minute. "For breaking up with you, first of all. But also for being a complete tool while I was doing it, too."

I raise myself up, putting my chin in my hand. "I think we've both suffered our fair share."

He frowns. "We shouldn't have, though. We should've just rode off into the sunset together, and never looked back."

I bite my lip, glancing away. "But if you weren't concerned for Asher, you wouldn't be you."

"You are too goddamned forgiving." He twines his fingers with mine, which only serves to remind me how much bigger he is than me. "Your brother probably won't be so nice."

I raise my eyebrows. "Asher? No, probably not. Although he has had his head up his own ass lately. He probably has zero idea that we're even... like..."

I trail off. Jameson kisses my neck, and I'm happy enough to let that particular topic of conversation fall by the wayside. I close my eyes as he sucks and bites my neck for a second.

"What did my brother do to get you so... mmm... devoted?" I ask.

The kisses stop as Jameson pauses for a second. "What do you mean?"

"I mean, like... I don't know. I figured that he must have helped you bury a body or something, the way you care what he thinks."

His brow furrows as he considers my words. "Asher didn't earn my loyalty by doing me a single favor. He did a whole series of them, from the day my grandma died until Gunnar went off to college. I think... I think maybe you missed some of the really hard stuff, like when I was trying to decide between feeding my brothers and making rent. And it was like that for *years*. I just kept thinking, this will be the day that this rich kid washes his hands of us. But he never did."

I bite my lip. "I had no idea that you felt that way, Jameson."

"Did you know that Asher helped me get my first bar backing job? Or an apartment, before I had enough credit? How about the time that he snuck us into the guest house so that I could save up some money? He literally saved us from starvation three times a year for almost ten years. And that's just the stuff I can put a dollar amount on... it doesn't include years and years of hearing me bitch about stuff that I found unfair."

I shake my head. "No, I didn't know about that. I'm guessing that you feel indebted to him still?"

He blows out a breath. "Yeah. I mean... how do you even start to pay that back? You can't, not really. All you can do is—"

"What you've been doing," I fill in, nodding. "Just being there, and being a good friend. I really do get that part, even if I don't necessarily agree with it."

He closes his eyes for a minute, running his hand through his short dark hair. "What else am I supposed to do? How do I repay that debt?"

I purse my lips. "Have you talked to Asher about it?"

He just shakes his head silently.

"Have you considered that he might not feel like you owe him some massive debt? He may feel that he gave you those things because he had them to give." I pause, thinking. "There's also the possibility that he may feel that he got something out of the deal, too. I know for a fact that you two got busted together for fighting on the playground plenty of times. I guarantee you that Asher's scrawny ass didn't do most of the fighting."

He smiles faintly at that, opening his dark eyes. "You should've seen how awkward he was as a middle schooler. Talking to girls was a real problem for him."

"And how did he get past that? My bet is that you had something to do with it."

"Maybe." He shrugs one shoulder. "That's still next to nothing, comparatively."

I sigh, letting the subject drop. I screw my face up, thinking.

"Can I ask you a weird question?"

He looks at me sideways. "Of course."

"When did you first look at me and think that I was hot?" I blush as I say it.

Jameson shifts me off of his chest and turns so that he's lying on his side. "That's a complex question."

"I don't mean it to be. I'm just curious when you noticed me. I will admit to having dirty thoughts about you as early as twelve or thirteen, probably."

His eyebrows shoot up. "Really?"

"Yeah. I know that you barely noticed me, but you were a fixture in my life for a really long time." I hope he's going to stay in my life for the foreseeable future and beyond... but I don't say it.

He is thoughtful. "Well... you're probably going to cringe, but I really only started paying attention to you around the time that Cure opened. You weren't really around me a lot before then, not day to day anyway."

"What? I like, lived for the times when I knew I was going to see you."

He shrugs. "I'm sorry. I was just wrapped up in my own stuff. If you didn't know, I had a lot going on then."

"Oh, you mean making sure that all your brothers got into college on scholarships wasn't a mindless activity for you?" I tease.

"Hah! No. Especially Gunnar. I swear, I thought he was going to be my personal downfall."

"Hmmm," I say. "You still didn't answer my original question, though. When was the first time that you saw me and thought that I was even vaguely attractive?"

He heaves a sigh. "Probably when you were seventeen."

My eyes go wide. "Seventeen?"

"Yep. I remember that you used to wear those cutoff denim overalls with a tube top... that will stick in my memory forever, even though I will probably burn in hell for it."

I grin. "I knew it! I definitely wore those teeny little shorts for your benefit, for your information."

Jameson grins. "Is that a fact?"

"Yeah, definitely. I was just waiting for you to like... notice me and sweep me off my feet. I had a very rich fantasy life when I was a teenager, I will tell you that much."

He leans down and kisses me on the lips, ever so slowly. "I definitely am glad that I didn't know any of that back then. You were jailbait, for sure."

I smile. "Are you saying that you wouldn't have gone to jail for me?"

"No, just the opposite. I would have, without hesitation." He noses my face to the side, tickling my neck with his facial hair.

"You would have made a pretty sexy jail bird though," I say with a giggle. He pulls me close and overpowers me, which I find thrilling.

He kisses his way down my neck to my collarbone. "Maybe you should tell me some of your teenage fantasies. You know, that way I can make sure that you are really, really happy with me."

"Oh yeah?" I ask, my pulse starting to race.

There is a wicked glint in his eyes. "Definitely. I want to make sure you're as content with me as possible. You know what they say. Happy girl, happy world."

He kisses his way down to my breasts, finding my nipples already standing at attention. He covers one soft pink areola with his mouth, sealing his lips over it and sucking hard.

White hot lightning shimmers through my whole body. I gasp, my back bowing. "You are wicked," I whisper.

He releases my breast and gives me a huge grin. "I try my best."

Then Jameson starts kissing his way downward, and we are lost in each other once again for hours and hours.

16

JAMESON

*A*fter we spend a whole twenty four hours exhausting each other, hardly leaving Emma's bedroom, I'm still starved for her. For her touch, yes. And her body.

But also for her laugh, for her way of excitedly telling stories. Her honesty. Her acceptance of me, flaws and all.

So I do what I've never done in my entire adult life... I actually call in sick to work. I call Forest and say that I'm not coming into Cure for the next two days. I don't say that I'm sick, just that I'm not coming in.

I think he is a little startled by my announcement, but Forest just says okay. When I hang up the phone, I look at Emma and think, *we need to go somewhere*. Not somewhere far. And not for too long.

I just feel the need to be somewhere else with Emma. Somewhere that's as wild and beautiful as she is, somewhere way outside the city.

Forsythe State Park pops into my head. It's an uninterrupted stretch of wild coastline that's only a couple of hours from here. I haven't been since I was a kid. I can imagine Emma walking along the cliffs on the shore, see her walking among the tall pine trees. In my mind she wears plaid and little booty shorts.

Yeah, I need to take her away for sure.

"Do you want to go away for a couple of days?" I ask her. "Today, I mean. I'm thinking we could go to Forsythe."

She looks up at me and gives me a sly smile. "Go on a mini-vacation with you? I guess I could do that."

I get out my ancient laptop and start looking for a cabin to stay in. Something with a nice fireplace, so I can end a long day of staring at Emma's amazing ass by stripping her down in front of the fire.

"Start packing," I tell her, getting up to get my credit card out of my wallet. "I'm booking this place right now."

She gets up and pulls on a pair of underwear and a t-shirt, then starts packing. I book a place on Air Bnb, then I kiss Emma and tell her I'll be right back.

It's only the work of a half an hour to run to my house and grab everything I will need. Within the hour, Emma is in the Jeep with me and we are speeding down the highway towards Forsythe State Park.

We've done nothing but talk and fuck for the last day, so it's nice to let the wind stream in as I drive. It's not silence exactly, but we are each able to be quiet. To live in our own thoughts.

She cracks open a book and reads most of the way. I'm busy taking in the sights when we get outside the city. The road starts rising little by little, and we drive alongside the rocky bluffs.

I glance over at Emma while we drive. She's lost in her book, chewing on a nail distractedly as she slowly turns the pages. The wind blows her hair every direction at once, but she still manages to take my damn breath away.

If I'm honest with myself, she always could. Always has.

There is just something about her that goes beyond her obvious beauty... there is something wise in her eyes. Something comforting in her smile. I don't want to rush things in any way, and we've only just gotten back together.

But she makes me feel something, deep inside. She not only

stirs my lust, but she damn well plucks the strings of my heart, too.

Damn, how did Emma manage to get herself so far underneath my skin?

Any way you slice it, I have vague plans for us in the future. I'm not exactly sure what they are, because a lot of it depends on Emma herself. But if I have my way, one day in the not-too-distant future she will be wearing my ring and calling herself Mrs. Hart.

There's a certain satisfaction in knowing that she would be mine forever. Knowing that I would never have to search for anything else, because I had Emma.

Of course, then I think about the whole idea of marrying into Emma's family — and Asher's family, too. I swallow, my mouth going dry. I've met their parents a handful of times, and none of those times they were particularly impressed with me.

Plus, there is the bit about her being in law school. She will barely have time to sleep and eat over the next two years, much less worry about the stress of being a bride.

So yeah, my fantasy of asking Emma to marry me might be a couple of years off. But the idea is still there, clutched tight to my chest.

I marvel at myself, at how much I want her, when a month ago I couldn't get far away enough. It definitely feels super strange to have all of these plans for the two of us, that's for sure.

I pull off the highway, exiting into a dense patch of trees. I follow the GPS on my phone which leads me to a little rutted trail. I can hear the beach from here, the rolling waves ceaseless as always. But I can't see anything yet except the tall pines, coming closer and closer together.

All at once, we break through the tree line. I'm a little shocked at how suddenly the path ends, the dark blue ocean splayed out right there, going on for miles and miles. The cabin is to the right, quaint and rustic with its dark wooden beams.

I pull up to the cabin just as Emma looks up from her book.

"Ohh," is all she says, looking out over the bluffs to the ocean. "Holy crap."

We get out of the Jeep, spending a few minutes getting our suitcases inside. The cabin is exactly what I wanted, the front room basically a ton of windows on one side and a bunch of places to lounge on the other. It even has the fireplace; I will definitely be stripping Emma bare in front of it later tonight.

"Let's go!" Emma says, pulling at my hand. "I want to explore."

She tows me toward the front door, and I let myself be led. I follow her out across the rocky bluff, to the very edge. She grips my hand as we both peer over.

"There's a little shore down there," she says, pointing to the tiny strip of shoreline between the bluffs and the swirling ocean.

I look down, frowning. Right now the swell of the sea was lapping gently twenty yards away, but I bet that wasn't always the case. "I bet that you wouldn't want to get caught there when the tide was about to shift. I imagine that you would be pressed right up onto the rocks."

She glances at me. "When will the tide shift?"

I glance up at the sun, trying to gauge its position in the sky. "I think maybe six hours from now? Give or take."

She grins triumphantly. "Can we go down there? I mean, I know that we will have to hike a while, but I think it'd be worth it."

"Yeah, definitely. Let's just make sure that we grab some water bottles before we go."

We go back to the house, where I grab the water bottles and she changes into yoga pants. I can't be mad about that. I have never seen her in workout gear before, but there is something about the way her ass moves in yoga pants that instantly has me hard as a rock. When I insist that she leads the way as we snake our way up a hiking trail that follows the rise of the bluffs, she is too eager to comply.

Soon enough though, she has me figured out.

"Are you even doing anything back there other than checking out my butt?" She looks back over her shoulder, pinning me with her gaze.

I glance up from her ass, unashamed. "Nope."

Emma sighs and drops back so that she's walking with me. The path that we've traveling narrows a little, and trees start to pop up, the foliage growing thicker pretty quickly.

She's quiet for a minute, but I can see the gears turns in her head. "Can I ask you a question?"

"Depends. Is it about Asher or Cure?"

She makes a face. "Neither. It's about your parents."

"My parents?" I ask, a little thrown off. "What about them?"

"I've just never heard you talk about them. What do you remember?"

I take a full minute to consider her question. "Well, they were young when they had me. My mom was probably about fifteen. She wasn't even twenty years old when Gunnar was born."

"Yeah?"

I nod. "My dad was a little older than her, but not by much. They were both addicted to heroin before we were born." I pause. "Gunnar was taken away by the state at birth because he tested positive for opiates when he was born. Don't tell him that, though."

"Wait, really?"

"Mmmhm. My grandma stepped in and took him, and then took in all three of us in the next few months."

"Wow, I had no idea. Do you remember your parents much?"

I screw up my face. "Kinda. I remember them arguing a lot. They got the cops called because they were both pretty violent towards each other. I remember being glad when they got their *medicine*, because they would be calm for a day then."

Emma takes my hand, lacing her fingers with mine. "I'm sorry."

I shrug. "It could've been worse. At least they didn't hit me or my brothers or anything."

"So you were shipped off to your grandmother's at... what, five?"

"Yep. Grandma Ruth. She was very strict, but she was around when we needed her. I didn't ever—" I stop, taking a breath. I wasn't really ready for this conversation to get all heavy. "I never told her while she was alive how much I appreciated that she took us in. She didn't have to."

She squeezes me hand. "I'm sure she knew."

I give Emma a tight smile. The path shifts and starts heading downward, and the trees thinning out. The path veers right and the trees vanish. Suddenly I'm looking at a view of the ocean.

Beneath my feet the ground starts to slope drastically, leading down to a long set of stairs that have been carved into the rock. We clatter down the stairs together, reaching the pebbled shore at the bottom.

I step out from the stone staircase, looking behind me with awe.

"We just climbed down that." I point at the towering stone bluff. "That seems impossible."

She slips her arm around my waist. "It's pretty cool down here. The water is so dark, and the rocks too. Then you've got this strip of sandy beach down the middle that provides a nice contrast."

I look down at Emma, taking in her wide green eyes, her dark hair, her angelic facial features. I get hard again, right then and there, without exactly knowing why.

"You know what would be nice?" I ask, brushing her hair away from her ear. I lean down and kiss her earlobe.

She seems a little surprised, but she's not even a little immune to the feel of my tongue tracing the shell of her ear. "No, what?"

I walk her backward so that she's pressed against the tall stone bluff. "We should fuck right here. Right now."

I grind my cock against her belly and groan into her ear.

Whatever I'm doing works on her, because she pulls my mouth down to hers, sighing as I kiss her.

"Don't make me wait," is all she says, wrapping her arm around my neck.

"Never," I solemnly promise. "You never have to wait again."

I kiss her and the sound of us fucking fades into the sound of the sea.

17

EMMA

I look at my phone, sighing silently. I'm at lunch with my mother, at a ridiculously fancy place... and I'm counting the minutes until we're done. I look around the dining room, look at the white linen tablecloths and waiters wearing white.

All I want is to not be wearing this tight pink dress and to be off with Jameson, but I had to leave his bed eventually. And my mother made it clear that I was going to attend this luncheon, so here I am.

It doesn't mean I have to be happy about it though.

"Can you believe that Sarah Perkins?" my mother sniffs, sipping her glass of white wine. "She came right out and made her opinions known. Though no one but her husband took her seriously. All the rest of us know that Nancy is from... well, let's just say, she didn't *come up* with wealth. And she still has a whiff of money grubbing poverty on her. It's plain enough to see."

I push my salmon around my plate, barely listening. "That's terrible."

"Isn't it? The woman is a harridan, that's for sure." She flags down a passing waiter. "Another glass of the pinot gris, please?"

My mother's disapproving gaze passes over me. "Are you just going to sit there all day moping?"

I straighten up. "What should I be saying?"

She shifts in her seat, smoothing a hand over her white dress. "I would like to know what happened on your date with Rich."

I flush, looking down. "Mom, Rich is really not a nice guy. He shoved me against a wall. He bruised my arms."

Her gaze narrows. "I don't see any bruises."

"That was a week ago!" I put my fork down and put my napkin on top of the plate. Almost instantly, a waiter steps in and removes the plate.

Another delivers my mother's fresh glass of wine. She inclines her head, but keeps her focus on me.

"I think you're being a little exciteable." She sips her wine.

"About the fact that he got very drunk and violent with me? I don't think so."

"Emmaline!" my mother says, looking around as if people heard me. "Keep your voice down. And I highly doubt that is actually what happened."

"That's exactly what happened." I keep my voice even, though I'm starting to seethe inside. "If you need proof, you can find it on the police report. He actually admitted it."

My mother rolls her eyes at me. "I hope that wasn't your doing."

I know my mom is a cold bitch sometimes, but I honestly cannot believe her right now. "The police hauled him away. If they are pressing charges, it's nothing to do with me. I was the victim, though."

I wrap my arms protectively around my torso, shooting my mother a glare.

My mother sighs. "Fine, fine. But just because you had a bad experience with Rich, that doesn't mean you just stop dating all together. Otherwise you'll be thirty before you know it, alone and bitter."

My jaw drops. "I can't believe you!"

"Nor I you, frankly." She sits back in her chair and swirls her wine. "I'm just trying to guide you to a husband. One would think you would be more grateful."

I grit my teeth. "As it so happens, I am seeing someone."

"Oh?" She sits up. "Who?"

"Someone who isn't part of your weird little group of your cronies' children. Someone who wouldn't be caught dead at one of your parties, as a matter of fact."

My mother's expression flattens.

"So you're just going to throw your life away and marry some nobody? No, I don't think so." She grabs her purse and pulls out her phone. "I'll start making calls for you right now. Evelyn Becker was just saying that her son is ready to settle down…"

"Mother—" I frown as she continues looking at her phone. I stand up and reach my hand over her screen. "Mom! Stop! Jesus christ."

She looks at me, affronted. "Emmaline, darling, I'm just trying to make sure you don't end up alone. It's a mother's duty to see her child is taken care of."

I blow out a breath. "I just told you I'm seeing someone. I'm not alone. And even if I was, I don't need you fixing me up anymore. Most of the kids of your friends are heinous, if you hadn't noticed."

"Oh, I don't know about that…"

"Well I do," I say, retaking my seat. "I'm sure that there are exceptions, but I don't really want to find out for myself. I'm perfectly happy."

My mother lifts a brow. "What is his name, this man that is supposedly wooing you? What does he do?"

I bite my lip, looking down. "It's still so new. I don't feel comfortable airing out all of his personal details to you yet."

She takes a sip of her wine. "It sounds like you've made someone up to put me off."

"He is real, I assure you."

"And you think that he will be able to support you when you graduate?"

I pause, confused. "What? I'll be able to work. Why wouldn't I just do that?"

My mother looks at me like I must be dumb. "You'll be pregnant, I presume. You won't have time for an actual *job*, Emmaline."

I want to protest. I even open my mouth, but nothing comes out. I don't doubt her sincerity… it's just that my mother lives in such a different world than I do.

"Mother," I say, not even knowing where to start. "First off, I am not going to magically get pregnant, unless I'm trying. Thank god for birth control. Second, I assume that you would prefer me to be married first…"

"That goes without saying."

"Right. Third, I plan on finding a job and holding that job, regardless of whether or not I am, in fact, pregnant. People do it all the time."

Her mouth puckers into a sour expression. "You think you can do it all, but you can't. Especially not right after a baby."

I feel a little sorry for her. "I don't think that. I do think that men should be active and involved in the child rearing process, though."

"Oh, really, Emmaline!" she says, exasperated. "That is just crazy talk. If your father heard you say that, he would ship you off to a rehab center."

"He'd have to get me declared mentally incompetent, then. Because I wouldn't go for no reason. And what you're saying, that we disagree over who would raise my theoretical child? That isn't an argument that Daddy could make to the court."

I stand up, grabbing my purse. I'm careful to brush the wrinkles out of my dress.

"Emmaline…"

"I have to go, mother. I have somewhere to be. Thank you for lunch." I turn and walk out of the dining room. I hope I look cool and collected, but inside I'm so outraged that I'm shaking.

I get outside of the restaurant, gulping lungfuls of fresh air. Usually I do a much better job of putting my hackles up, but today I let my mother really get my goat.

Once I pull myself together, I drive home in my coupe. The Range Rover that I had for a few days was nice, but it was just a loaner while my car was serviced. I zip my little car in and out of lanes, mindlessly driving toward home.

I try not to steam over the horrible stuff my mother said, really I do. I breathe deeply, I count to fifty, I do all the woo woo stuff that a therapist once recommended when dealing with my family. It doesn't lessen the sting, though.

When I get home, I'm still so in my head that I almost pass by Evie and Maia. I back myself up, entering the kitchen to find the two of them sitting across from each other at the kitchen table. They're each gripping a mug of tea.

Apparently Evie has a method when she soothes a girl.

Maia wipes away a tear, looking away from me. Evie looks at me, her expression perfectly blank.

"What's going on in here?" I ask, curious.

"We're just talking." Evie sighs, sitting back in her chair.

I glance at Maia. "Boy stuff?"

Maia gives me a miserable nod. When she speaks, her highborn British accent is particularly strong. "Men suck."

I can't disagree with that. "You wanna get some takeout? A pizza, maybe?"

Evie lights up. "I'm starving."

I smile at her. "How about I go change, and then I meet you two on the porch? All you have to do is decide on toppings."

Evie grins and Maia gives me a watery smile. I scoot to my bedroom, changing into a denim miniskirt and an oversized blue tee. Then I grab my wallet and my phone and head to the porch.

Evie and Maia are curled up in the seats, so I take a seat on the floor.

"Are you two okay with that pizza place on Third? I dream of their breadsticks sometimes," I say.

"Sure," Maia says with a shrug.

Evie looks thoughtful. "I'm thinking goat cheese and sundried tomatoes..."

"Yes! And... anrtichokes!" Maia says.

"With a pesto base?" I ask.

"You know how much I love pesto," Evie says.

"Yeah, sounds perfect." Maia squints into the sunlight. "And breadsticks, because apparently this place has good ones."

"Oooh, and Diet Coke if they have it!" Evie says.

"You guys don't even know how much better you're making my day right now," I say, looking up the pizza place online. "After what a shitty morning I had, I'm living for this pizza order, I swear."

"Don't even get me started on having a bad morning," Maia mutters. "Did I already mention that boys suck so hard?"

"What happened?" I ask, a little distracted by the phone in my hands.

"My boyfriend... well, he's definitely an ex now, I guess. Anyway, he took a bribe from my family and ratted me out." Maia looks like she might throw up.

"Whoa, about what?" I ask.

Maia bites her lip. "I might have kind of... told my parents that I've been in art school this entire time? Like, getting my master's degree in fine arts?"

I look up from my phone, nothing short of shocked. "You what?"

She gives me a lopsided smile. "Your reaction is sure to be better than my parent's reaction. Anyway, I definitely don't want to talk about it. Definitely definitely *definitely*."

I shake my head a little, hitting the *order now* button on my phone. Then I focus on Maia. "Okay. But how does that affect your citizenship? I assume that you're here on a student visa…"

"Can we please not talk about this right now?" she begs.

Evie clears her throat. "How about we go back to man bashing? Cause men really really suck."

My phone vibrates gently in my hand. I look down and see a notification of a text from Jameson.

Busy?

With that one word, I'm smiling. I text him back.

Yes. Later, though?

I stifle a grin at his reply. *You know it.*

"Who is she getting text messages from that makes her smile?" Maia asks Evie, frowning.

"No one!" I insist, putting my phone down. "And the pizza is on the way. Now where were we with the man hating stuff?"

Evie gives me an odd look, but lets it go. And I just sit there and listen to them complain about the men that have screwed them over… all while secretly glowing from the inside out. Because even though my parents enrage me and my brother does things that I just don't understand…

Jameson is there for me. He is steadfast this time, in it for the long haul. I can feel it.

And that means that I can't complain anymore. Not about him, at least.

18

JAMESON

"Are you sure we really need to go?" I ask, plucking at the hem of Emma's clingy black dress. I'm sprawled on her bed, dressed in an expensive suit. "We could just stay in this bed, you know."

She looks down at me, grinning as she puts in a diamond earring. "It's your fancy Bartender's Guild thing that we're going to! You definitely have to go. Besides, you promised that we could go together, to test out… you know, being *out* together."

I reach up and grab her, pulling her on top of me. I put my lips to her ear, shaping her hips through her dress. "I can think of ten things I would rather be doing."

For a second, she allows it. She puts her hands on my chest as I nibble on her earlobe, making a few breathy sounds.

"Mmmm," she says. "You are terrible."

I skim my hand up beneath her dress, slipping a couple of fingers into the waist of her panties. "There are some things that I am excellent at, I would say."

Her breath catches as my touch trails down to the crotch of her panties. I kiss her full mouth, trying to suppress the amusement I feel. I'm right, after all.

"Evil, is what you should be called." Her words come out stilted.

I yank her dress up to the waist, tugging her panties down. "You know you love it."

Emma looks at me, her eyes heavy lidded and full of lust. "This isn't going to make me change my mind about going tonight."

"We'll see," I say, kissing her lightly. Then I smack her ass. "I want you to ride my face until you cum."

"Oh, Jameson—" she starts to protest. I just smack her ass again.

"Too much talking, not enough writhing. Get the fuck up here, before I lose my temper."

She blushes ten shades of red, but she does move up the bed. She straddles my face, her movements hesitant. I turn my head and kiss her inner thigh, my facial hair tickling her bare skin.

She breathes heavily and cups her own breasts. I brace her by laying one hand on her bare ass and one hand on her lower abdomen. She smells so fucking good like this, with her legs on either side of my head. Using two fingers to lift and separate her lower lips, I find her already drenched with lust.

"Mmmm," I say as I reach my tongue out, teasing her pussy with light licks.

She moans and presses herself down, seeking more contact. I give it to her, swirling my tongue around her clit.

"I— I—" she says, her eyes closed tightly. "Fuckkkkk, that's so good."

I chuckle, the vibrations filtering into her body. For a while, I tease her by using my tongue to fuck her. She groans in frustration, and I grin. I shouldn't be enjoying this so much, but her impatient noises and the fact that she's creaming on my fucking tongue are just too damned good.

I seal my lips over her clit, sucking with long, hard pulls. Emma shatters on my face, squirting and pulsing. It's so fucking hot to see her like that, completely undone. I almost wish that I was inside her, but I know that everything has its time and place.

I just help her ride out the orgasm, licking lazily until she pulls away. She topples over away from me, breathing hard. I sit up, wiping her cum off of my face.

"Oh my god," she says, her eyes still closed.

Her dress is still around her waist. I take a moment to skim her hips and appreciate how wet her pussy still is, her wetness having spread out a little. I can see it gleaming in the dying daylight streaming in the window.

"God you're hot," I murmur, kissing her thigh.

She cracks open an eye. "You make me crazy. That final move you did where you sucked on my clit?" She makes a strangled sound. "That will be the death of me, I'm sure of it."

My lips curl upward. "Seems like a good way to go."

Emma sighs. "Will you pass me my panties?"

I cock my head. "I think not. The idea of you being bare under that dress all night is probably the only way you're going to trick me into going to this damned thing."

Her eyebrows rise, but she doesn't insist on it. She just pushes herself up off the bed, working her dress down over her hips. She smoothes it down like I didn't just make her cum everywhere a couple of minutes ago.

She starts to walk to the closet, but I grab her and kiss her on the butt. She resists, struggling a little. I pay her no mind, burying my face down between her ass cheeks.

"I think that later I'm going to eat your ass, and you're going to love every second of it. So think about that all night while we're socializing."

Then I release her, standing up. She turns around and looks at me, seeming a little dazed and a little petrified.

"You like doing that?" she asks.

"I like the fact that you will come harder than you've ever come before. And I like getting you comfortable with having your ass played with. Eventually, I plan to cum in it, but you have to start small. So that's a hell of a bonus." I wink, moving to get my shoes.

She just stares at me, her jaw hanging open. "You are fucking insane."

"Come on, let's get moving. We're already late, thanks to you being so needy," I tease.

"You are the worst!" she tells me as she gets her shoes on. "Just so you know that."

I usher her out of her room and hurry her to my car. By the time we get all the way to downtown and hustle ourselves inside the hushed, darkened interior of the bar where the event is being held, it's almost dark outside. The Golden Compass, the bar in question, is high-end and nautical themed, draped sumptuous ruby carpet and navy leather booths. It's got a gold countertop that runs the length of the bar, and a matching gold backsplash behind that, with many kinds of fine rum on display.

I take Emma's hand, wandering forward into the bar. We are late, for sure; a couple of the bartenders are talking to the group about setting up a wine tasting. There's barely any room left behind the last couple of bartenders to cram in, but my height and size make people shift over enough that we both fit in.

One of the guys who's talking to the group, looks over my way. He's so hip, he's almost dressed like a circus performer, complete with the handlebar mustache. "Well, well! Look who made it."

Heads turn to take in my presence. I elbow my way through the crowd, making sure that Emma stays with me. I shake hands with him.

"Jethro, man. I don't know if I have already told you, but I love this space."

"Thanks, man. Who is your lady?" He looks at Emma, who blushes furiously.

"This is Emma. Emma, this is Jethro, who owns the bar that we're standing in."

"Nice to meet you," she says, all politeness.

"We were just talking about doing a wine tasting. We could split it up among different bars, maybe do a cheese plate with it too," Jethro says. "Beth, what were you saying?"

He turns to Beth, who is dressed like a 90s raver. These people are too cool for school, that's for sure.

"Oh, just that we could do a special night, or we could have like… a special menu that's available for a week." She looks very intent.

"Right. What do you guys think? A week, or a special night?" Jethro asks the crowd.

"How about a month?" someone in the back calls out.

"I second that!" a woman says.

I look to Emma, checking up on her. She smiles a little, and I squeeze her hand. She is easy in that way; she knows that this is my world, and she seems perfectly happy to take a back seat and let me drive. At the same time, it's not like most of the meeting is over her head or totally uninteresting.

She's just willing to take it all in. I appreciate that more than she knows.

Later, when most of the crowd has dispersed, Emma and I sit pressed close together on one of the bench seats. There's a table in front of us, and Beth is going on at length about buying the wood barrels that whiskey is aged in.

Jethro comes over with a small tray of rum cocktails, all festively decorated with pineapple slices and tiki umbrellas. He puts them down in front of us. "Try our new drink. It's like a Mai Tai, but more refreshing. It's made with a ton of coconut juice."

I sip my drink, making a satisfied sound. I raise an eyebrow at Emma. "What do you think?"

She puts the straw to her lips, closing her eyes as she samples it. Her eyes snap open, fiercely green.

"You should bottle this and sell it to sorority girls. You'd sell a million cases, no problem," she declares.

Jethro chuckles. "I'm glad that you like it."

"Mmm," she says demurely.

I slide my hand under the table, gripping Emma's bare knee. She looks at me, still sipping. There is a naughty sparkle in her eyes. I edge my hand upward, closer to her body.

This flirting with someone I'm meant to flirt with thing is new for me. It's a novel experience to bring to an event someone who I respect and whose clothes I want to rip off later.

Is this what being in an actual relationship is like? If so, it's not bad.

Not that Emma and I have made anything official... I glance at her. If Emma has had time to see anyone else though, I would be very surprised. We've been inseparable for the last two weeks.

"Do you serve mainly rum drinks here, then?" Emma asks Jethro.

Jethro puffs up, launching into what is obviously a carefully practiced speech about why he has a bar that caters to rum lovers. I try not to roll my eyes when he debuts the term proto-tiki. He's just excited that someone asked him, is all.

When Jethro gets up to have us try another drink, I lean down to Emma's ear. "I'm going to do dirty things to you soon. You know that, right?"

She looks up at me with an expression of amusement that says *bring it on*. I sip my drink and put twenty minutes on my mental timer. In twenty minutes, we'll make our excuses and leave.

And then the real fun begins.

19

EMMA

When we get back to my house, at my door, he's undressing me even before I get the door unlocked. The second we're inside, he picks me up and carries me into my bedroom. Jameson sets me down and sits back on my bed.

He looks me up and down, his gaze dark and piercing. It seems like he sees right into my very soul. I feel almost shy, like I should have worn more than this skimpy dress, but it doesn't matter. He grabs my hands when I try to cover myself, then pulls me onto his lap.

"Do you have any idea how fucking hot you are?" he growls into my ear. I moan and shift to straddle his big body, moving closer any way I can.

I flush hot all over. Straddling him like this, it's impossible not to feel his hardened cock through his jeans. It feels long and thick and perfect. I get a flash of how good it will feel inside my pussy, stretching me out and making me writhe in ecstasy.

"Maybe," I whisper. The air in the room feels too hot on my skin, too heavy.

"You definitely don't," he says, sliding his hand into my hair and bringing me down to meet his lips. I enjoy the little bit of pain as he grips my hair, controlling me.

I kiss him, enjoying the warmth rising up from his body. He moves down to kiss my neck, which makes me shudder with pleasure. He squeezes one of my breasts, his movements lazy and slow. My body burns for his, the fire spreading first between my breasts and then down between my legs.

I rock my hips against his, craving his touch. My breasts, my ass, my pussy… they're all aflame, and his magic touch is the only thing that will soothe the insistent burn. I slide my hand down my belly. He sucks in a breath as my hand creeps down between our bodies.

"Not so fast," he says, using his grip on my hair to pull my head back. "I want you to get off my lap and get naked."

I bite my lip, pushing off of him. He releases my hair and gets up.

"Good girl," he says. "Now get naked. And sit on the edge of the bed. I'll be right back."

He disappears, leaving me to strip down. I take off my dress, shimmying out of it and dropping it to the floor. I hesitate, then unhook my bra and take that off. I wait for a second to see if Jameson will reappear, but he doesn't.

So I take a seat on the bed, placing my ass on the very edge of the bed. He comes back in the room, a silky black bag in his hands. He closes the door behind himself, giving me a wicked smile. He sets the bag down beside me and looks at me, like a big cat contemplating his prey.

His eyes are everywhere on my naked skin. They feel like a caress, hot and heavy. He opens the shiny black bag, withdrawing a popsicle, lube… and a smooth purple dildo, about three inches long. My eyes go wide.

"A dildo?" I say. The very idea of him using that on me makes me squirm. "Aren't you supposed to want to be the only dick in this bedroom?"

"Cute." He grins. He tosses the dildo on the bed, pulling his t-shirt off over his head. He looks appreciatively at my naked body, at my perky nipples.

"Don't worry about that right now," he says, coming over to stand between my legs. "Just be with me, Emma."

He tears the wrapper off the popsicle, revealing the flavor. It is bright cherry red. He puts his mouth on it, mmming a little for my benefit. The he pulls it out of his mouth with a pop, holding it out to me. I hesitantly stick out my tongue, shivering at how cold and sweet it is.

He kneels down on the floor between my knees, sucking on the popsicle. I can't help but stare at him, at the way his mouth and throat work as he sucks on the popsicle so intently.

"It's sweet," he says, his eyes full of dark promise. "But not as sweet as you."

He kisses me, the fruity flavor of the popsicle still on his tongue. Then he pulls back, brushing the popsicle over the tip of my breast. I gasp. He follows the cold of the popsicle with the heat of his mouth, using his tongue.

I moan, vaguely aware of how needy he's making me, and thrust my chest out. The hot and cold sensations are so opposite, raising goosebumps across my skin. I can feel everything so much more sharply, with laser precision, as he abrades my nipple with his tongue.

I cry out. He pushes me back on the bed, bringing the popsicle down lower. I buck once, and he stops and looks up at me.

"Don't move. Don't make a sound, or I will stop. Do you understand?"

My oversexed brain make me sit up and stare at him like an idiot.

"am I not clear?" he says.

"No, you were," I say.

"Good. That's the last I want to hear from you," he says, pushing me back down. He kisses my inner thigh, and I have to grip the sheets, trying desperately not to squirm or moan.

His tongue follows the popsicle to my belly button, to my hip bone, then down between my legs. I bite my lower lip, struggling to lie still. By the time he brushes the popsicle over my clit, I am ready to scream from the anticipation he has built up inside me.

The popsicle disappears, tossed aside somewhere. He knows my body, he knows that I'm ready to burst. He takes his time about making me cum though. He slowly licks and sucks at my clit until I am panting, trying not to beg as he wrings every last drop of pleasure from my flesh.

He stops for a second, and I audibly whine. He moves to retrieve the dildo. I freeze up a little but before I can protest, he returns to lick my clit in slow, lazy circles.

I am desperate for him, moaning and clenching my hands into fists in the sheets. He takes full advantage, easing the dildo against my lower lips. I am so wet and excited that I don't need any lube. As he presses the dildo against my pussy I make a sound, a kind of whimper, and he takes his mouth away again.

I could feel my body weeping for him, feel the sheets beneath my body growing damp, clinging to my ass cheeks.

"Are you going to be a good girl and be quiet so that I can finish eating your pussy?" he murmurs against my bare flesh. "I really hope you are, because I can't wait to watch you call out my name."

I nod, feeling my face grow red. I shut my mouth and go still, willing him to continue.

He presses against my pussy lips again with the dildo. I am so wet, it slides in partially with no resistance. God, the pressure of the dildo feel good, almost like his cock.

He withdraws it, kissing my clit once more. I couldn't be quiet, so I groaned softly. He doesn't pause, he just moves the dildo in again, licking my clit.

"Oh god," I gasp. "Fuck!"

I grab the sheets, knowing that I am going to come soon. I feel my thighs shake as he french kisses my clit. As he moves his tongue, he gently pulls the dildo out of my pussy, and moves it to my ass instead.

I am shocked enough by the contact to make a noise, but luckily this time he doesn't stop licking. He turns up the intensity of his french kiss as he gently presses the dildo against my ass.

Jameson pauses, and I groan. When he returns, he moves the little dildo against my rear entrance once more, and I feel the slipperiness of the lube he has added. I bite my lower lip and close my eyes.

It feels so naughty but so fucking good. He slips the dildo into my ass while he kisses my clit. The sensation of being very full and very fucking ready to come washes over me.

"Oh god... please..." I beg him.

He chuckles. That is enough for me. My eyes roll back in my head, and I clench and shake. I feel enraptured, but even as I am drifting down, he is already preparing for more. He sheds his jeans, his expression intense.

He gets up, putting the dildo aside. Flipping me over on my hands and knees, he smacks my ass once. A chill runs down my spine, unbidden,

Jameson actually growls his excitement, which only increases my sense of anticipation. He pushes my thighs apart and presses his thick cock against the entrance to my pussy. He feels so huge from this angle, impossibly big.

He uses a little of my lubrication to push himself halfway in. We both groan. He wraps my long dark hair in his fist, withdraws slightly, and then hammers himself home.

I cry out, the pleasure bordering on pain. He is so big, filling every single inch of me, touching every secret spot inside.

He grasps one of my hips and starts thrusting slowly. I shudder as he withdraws and then fills me completely, again and again. Jameson increases his speed, gripping my hair and fucking me harder.

I moan, feeling him filling every inch of my pussy. He shifts a little, and suddenly he is hitting my g-spot. I tighten and clench instinctively around his cock.

"Ah!" I call. "God, right there!"

"You like that?" he growls. "I want you to cum so hard. I want to feel you cream all over my cock."

I groan as he hits my g-spot over and over, his thrusts as rapid as gunfire. Everything inside my body tightens.

"Oh god... oh god, Jameson, I'm— I'm—" I cry, clenching around his cock. I feel like I am exploding, my eyes rolling back in my head.

He groans as he comes, finishing with a final thrust. I can actually feel the hot spurts of cum as he releases them in my pussy.

"Fuck," he mumbles, struggling for breath.

He loosens his hold on my hair, leaning forward to kiss my lower back. I collapse on the bed, giving a breathless chuckle.

He withdraws, falling onto the bed beside me. I sweep my hair over my shoulder and roll over, facing him. He grabs my hand and kisses my knuckles.

As he lies there next to me, trying to control his breathing, I can't help the way my heart squeezes. When I look at him, I can hardly breathe for wanting to spill my guts all over the damn place.

Instead of telling him that I love him, though, I opt for temperance.

"Would it be weird if I asked you to be my boyfriend?" I blurt out. I turn red immediately, and it's all I can do to keep myself from covering my mouth.

He opens his eyes, his dark gaze pinning me. "It definitely wouldn't be weird. I would have asked you to be my girlfriend sooner or later, officially."

He props himself up on one hand, leaning forward to kiss me ever so slowly. My heart rate goes through the roof.

"Yeah?" I ask, feeling needy and pathetic. The part of me that worshipped Jameson for so long can't believe that I'm here right now, having this conversation with him.

He chuckles. "Yes. I feel…" He clears his throat, sobering. "It feels like we are more than boyfriend and girlfriend, though. There isn't a word for what we are, I feel like. I'm… I'm not even sure how this happened, to tell you the truth."

I kiss him, tasting the salt on his lips. "We'll have to make up a word, maybe."

His eyes crinkle. "Yeah."

"I'll work on it," I promise, snuggling closer.

He doesn't say anything, just holds me close. And that is plenty for me right now.

20

JAMESON

I worked late last night, which means that Emma spent the night in my bed. I wake up early the next morning and leave her sleeping peacefully in my bed, the sun only just creeping in the window. I spend a long while looking through my realtor's website, looking at prices and saving the properties that I like.

I might not be buying this house with Asher, but Forest did light a fire under my ass. Real estate is the way of the future, it seems. So I talked with a realtor about a week ago, and now she has me on her website, trying to figure out what I want.

I want at least two bedrooms. One for me, one for guests, or maybe an office. Also, I'd like a nice yard, big enough that I can grill in. Big enough for a nice swing set, some day in the distant future.

It seems kind of weird to be planning for something years ahead of time, but I'm doing it anyway. When I finally get a list of places that I want to see together, I email them to my realtor. Almost instantly, she responds asking if I have time to see them today.

Today? I try not to panic. I mean, I do have the day off today.

All I was going to do was try to convince Emma to surf. I think about it for a minute, then put my laptop aside.

Heading back to my bedroom, I creep in. Emma stirs in the bed, her long dark hair splayed out on her pillow. For a moment, I admire her dark lashes against her pale cheek, the soft petal pink of her lips.

I sit down beside her, and the movement makes her open her eyes a little. She sees me, and she smiles. Something stirs deep inside me, something raw and emotional.

"Hey you," she whispers.

"Hey." I lean down to kiss her, and she rises to meet my lips.

After a moment, she breaks away. "Is there a reason why you are already up?"

The corner of my mouth lifts. "Yeah, actually. How do you feel about looking at houses today?"

She seems surprised. "You mean, houses for you?"

"For me to buy," I clarify. "And live in."

Emma sits up. "I had no idea that you were even looking."

"I'm not, but I think I should change that." I glance at the sheet that she has tucked under her arm, to protect her modesty. It's barely hanging on. I tug it just a little, and I'm rewarded by seeing her full, pert breast.

"Jameson!" she scolds, plucking at the sheet.

I reach out and cup her breast, my fingers finding the nipple and tugging it gently. She looks irritated, but her nipple pebbles under my touch. When I bend down and take that pouty pink nipple in my mouth, she makes a soft sound.

Her fingers find my hair, playing with it lightly as I abrade her nipple with my tongue. Her eyes close part of the way.

"You are so bad," she says.

I suck on her flesh just a second longer, then release her. I left a nice bright pink mark on her areola, which I like seeing.

"You didn't answer my question, though." I slide my hand over her side, down her hip.

"About going to look at houses? Yes, of course I'll go. I love looking at an unfinished space." Her eyes open, more green than ever. "What time should we go?"

I'm distracted by pulling the sheet away from her body, though. "Later."

I get a good grip on her hips and kiss my way down her body. For a good long while, I'm lost in her throaty purrs and sighs of pleasure.

When my brain winds down again enough that I can think of the realtor once more, the sun is blindingly bright coming through the windows of my bedroom. I dig around for my phone and email her back, letting her know that today is good for me.

A couple hours later, Emma and I are standing in the front yard of a ranch home, holding hands and blinking into the sun. The house itself is unimpressive and bland, and the yard we are standing in is mostly sand and dirt.

"This home is great!" crows Ally, our middle aged realtor. She tugs on the hem of her too-short bright red power suit. "Two bedrooms, two baths. A recently remodeled kitchen. You guys just have to see the inside."

I just grunt, unsure about the suitability of the house so far.

Emma nudges me with an elbow. "We would love to see it."

Ally grins broadly and walks up to the front porch, wrestling with a lockbox on the front door. She grimaces as she pushes the door, which only opens with a long scraping sound. "You can see that this house is sort of a handyman's special. It has a lot of potential, but it's priced really reasonably…"

Emma glances at me. "This is your show. Do you want to go in?"

I hesitantly nod. "Yeah, I guess so."

I lead Emma inside, blanching a little at the green wallpaper and orange shag carpeting that greet us. It's straight out of the late seventies.

"This is a great starter home," Ally says. "It just needs some love and attention to be beautiful."

I clear my throat. "Are most of the homes in my price range so... in need of work?"

Ally smiles. "Not all of them. This one needs more work, but it's also bigger than a lot of the places on your list. Come in a little further and look around. I think you'll find that the house has really good bones."

We drift through the house while Ally describes how the kitchen has been remodeled, how the bedrooms can look amazing with very little work. The bathrooms are hilariously out of date, but there is enough space for an office. Plus there is a pretty large back yard, which could easily house the grill and swingset that I envision.

Ally leaves us alone in the back yard for a bit. Emma looks at me, curious.

"You haven't really said much the whole time. What do you think about this house?" she asks.

"I don't know," I say, sighing and running my hand through my hair. "Ally keeps talking about how much potential the house has, but I have trouble seeing it. What do you think?"

"Me? I don't know." She bites her lip.

I look at her. "You have an opinion, Emma. It could very well be your house, in a not too distant future. Can you imagine living here?"

She flushes bright pink. "Is that what you think?"

"What?"

She looks down at the ground. "That this could be my house some day."

I hesitate, confused. "Well, yeah. I'm asking your opinion because it actually matters whether or not you could see yourself settle in here someday soon. Moving in is the next step, isn't it?"

"It is..." she says, but she still won't look at me.

"Emma," I say, gently grasping her wrist. She looks at me, seeming conflicted. "Am I crazy in thinking that we'll eventually want to take that next step together?"

Her eyes mist over as she looks at me. When she speaks, her voice is a little choked up. "You are definitely not crazy. I just… I'm just happy to hear that you feel the same way, I guess."

I draw her in, closing my arms around her. "Of course I do. I might be a stubborn ass, but I feel like… like since we got past the whole being broken up thing… I don't know, I just thought…"

She presses her face against my chest, nodding. "I understand, I think. You feel like we'll just keep going, now that we cleared that one big hurdle."

"Exactly. That's it exactly." I couldn't say it myself, but she knew what I meant anyway. I can't express my gratitude enough through words, so I just hug her harder.

We stand like that for a while, her face pressed into me, my arms around her shoulders. Eventually Ally sticks her head out of the back door.

"Are you guys doing all right out here? Do you want to see some more houses?" she asks.

I pull back, looking down at Emma. The corners of her lips lift upward.

"I think we're ready to see another house. Right?" I ask.

She doesn't skip a beat or break eye contact. "Definitely ready."

"Great! I have another house that may be more up your alley," Ally chirps. "It definitely has more curb appeal than this house, for sure."

I take Emma by the hand, leading her through the house and out the front door. She is all smiles as we get in Ally's car and drive to the next house.

We drive until we're only a few blocks from Redemption Beach. I look at the sandy yards of the little bungalows with the white picket fences we're passing, my interest piqued. When we pull up out front of the place, I stare at the house for a full second.

It's a tiny cottage that's been painted bright yellow, with a neatly maintained sandy yard and a perfect white picket fence.

"Isn't it great?" Ally asks, looking back at me. "It's from the 1930s, all original inside too. And it's obviously on this super cute street of houses."

"I… it is great," I say, getting out of the car. I feel Emma as she gets out behind me. "This is what I imagine, when I imagine a house I could buy."

"Wait until you see the inside!" Ally says. "It looks cute as a postage stamp out here, but inside it's roomy, too."

Emma slips her hand into mine, squeezing my fingers. I follow Ally through the fence and into the yard.

"You're going to like the back yard area too," Ally says as she unlocks the door. "It's nice and big. It's even shaded by a couple of big trees."

Ally steps inside, opening the door into a sunny living room. The whole place is bare, but it's not hard to imagine it full of furniture. A couch by the wall, bookshelves on either side of the window. I guarantee that I look like a little fool, standing there with my mouth agape, letting my mind run away with me.

"Whoa," I say, because that's all that comes to mind. I look at Emma, and find her smiling.

"This place… this is cute," she says, releasing my hand to walk past the living room.

I am right on her heels, walking into an in between space, followed by the all-white kitchen. The bedrooms and bathroom branch off the in between room. The ceilings aren't that tall, maybe only a foot taller than me in some places, but I am willing to overlook that.

Emma pushes open the French doors that lead into the back yard. She looks back at me with such a joyful expression. "It's perfect."

And it is. There is a patio area with a fire pit in the middle on one side, and a big open area on the other side. As promised, there are two big shady trees in the back yard, arching over everything.

"You can almost see yourself throwing a party here," Emma murmurs.

"Or putting together a swing set right over here," I say, pointing to the empty area. Emma and I trade glances, her eyes widening a little.

"You think so?" she says, flushing a little.

I glance at Ally. "This is the one."

"Jameson—" Emma says. "It's the second place you've seen. Be reasonable."

I look her dead in the eye, unwavering. "When I see what I want, I'm going to get it. Once I've made up my mind about something, that's it. There isn't even any point in discussing it."

Emma blushes bright red, catching my double meaning easily. "You should still look around a little. Sleep on it for a few days."

I grab her by the waist, drawing her close so that I can kiss her lips, slow and sensual. Emma squirms a little because Ally is here, but I refuse to bend, holding her in place. When I release her lips, she's a little breathless.

I look down into her eyes. "It's decided."

She peers up at me. "Is it?"

I give her another kiss, then turn her loose. I look to Ally.

"I have to call my finance guy, but this is the house."

She looks surprised, but pleased. "Okay. This is the house! Yay!"

Emma and I follow her back through the house, and I feel immensely satisfied.

21

EMMA

Jameson rolls over in my bed in the middle of the night, rousing me. "Hey. Wake up."

"Hmmm?" I ask, drowsy. My eyes are closed, though I'm not fully asleep yet. He only let me go to sleep half an hour ago, but obviously I'm the only one who did a lot of resting. "What?"

"I have to tell you something, and I need you to be totally awake when I do." His voice is low and urgent.

I crack my eyelids, looking at him. He looks messy and yummy, if only I wasn't quite so exhausted. Actually, now that I think about it, *he* looks tired too. "Are you okay?"

He smiles, but he seems nervous. "Yeah. I just... I love you."

His words steal my breath away. I stare at him for a second, trying to decide if my sleep addled brain made up this little bit of fantasy or not. J looks uncomfortable for a second.

"Are you going to say anything?" he asks.

"I— Are you sure?" I ask. I desperately want to tell him that I love him, but only if he's one hundred percent certain.

He frowns. "Am I sure? What kind of question is that? Of course I'm sure."

My eyes immediately well up, and my voice grows thick. "You're really, totally sure?"

J wraps his arm around my waist, pulling me close. "Absolutely, completely, totally sure. I love you, Emma. I think I have loved you for longer than I care to admit, even to myself."

"Oh my god," I whisper, my eyes overflowing. "I love you too. I've loved you since I was old enough to know what love was, I think."

I press my lips to his, aware of the tears flowing down my face. His taste is so familiar to me by now, and I find that more comforting than anything.

He rolls me over so that I'm on top of him, and I straddle him. Even as I cry happy tears, I pull his cock inside me, riding him as intensely as I know how.

He kisses away my tears as best he can and thrusts up inside me, using his hand to rub my clit. We come together, crying out, emboldened by the words we've just learned to say to one another.

As Jameson and I lie together, our breathing still ragged, I test out the new phrase.

"I love you," I whisper into his jaw.

He looks at me. "And I love you."

I slowly drift off to sleep with a smile on my face.

It's just dinner with Gunnar, I tell myself nervously. As Jameson leads me into the casual dining restaurant, I straighten my skirt and try to remind myself to play it cool.

I look around at the brightly painted walls and the many leather booths. The hostess brightens when she sees Jameson and waves us on into the dining room. Apparently Jameson and his brothers know this Mexican place pretty well.

"Hey, you two," Gunnar says, sprawled out in one of the back booths. His eyes drop to where Jameson holds my hand, widening for just a moment.

Jameson doesn't skip a beat, moving to sit across from his brother. I scoot into the booth, my cheeks turning red.

"Hey Gunnar," I greet him.

Gunnar looks between us. "You're an item then, huh?"

Jameson stretches his arms out, putting one around me. He's visibly tense. "Yep. Is that going to be a problem?"

"With me? Nope." Gunnar grins. "Mazel Tov."

Jameson relaxes a little. "Okay then."

I pick up my menu. "Are their margaritas any good here? I think we could all use one."

Jameson gives me an appreciative squeeze. "They're excellent."

The waiter comes over and Jameson orders a pitcher of margaritas on the rocks. We also all order food, and I opt for the chicken fajitas.

"That sounds good. Can I get those too, but with steak?" Jameson asks.

Gunnar goes for a ground beef burrito with mole sauce. When the waiter immediately returns with our margaritas, there is some shuffling and pouring. It's funny how the two brothers divide and conquer the smallest task, with Gunnar setting up the glasses and Jameson meting out a little of the yellowish liquid into each glass.

"Thanks," I say when Gunnar hands me my glass.

I sit back, taking a sip. I pucker a little, as the liquid is both sweet and sour. It's also got a pretty strong tequila taste.

Gunnar sips his and sighs, audibly contented. He looks between us, as if trying to figure something out.

"What?" I ask.

"Nothing," he says with a shake of his head. He looks hesitant.

I glance at Jameson, who is studying Gunnar's face.

"Spit it out. I can tell that you want to say something." Jameson pushes his margarita around on the table top.

Gunnar pulls a face, leaning forward. He motions to the two of us. "How long have you guys been... you know, doing *this*?"

"Two months. Almost three by now, I guess." Jameson says it with his voice full of contempt, like he's expecting Gunnar to start a fight.

Under the table, I put my hand on Jameson's knee. We exchange glances, and I try to silently tell him to take it easy.

"Does Asher know?" Gunnar asks. When we don't answer right away, he sort of shakes his head. "Of course not. He would go ape shit if he did. Not that I'm saying that is reasonable, but..."

"You're the first person we're telling together," I cut in, to stem the flow of angry words that I'm sure Jameson wants to unleash. "You're like the starter home, and Asher is like the big lavish mansion. You know, baby steps."

Gunnar nods, his brows knitting. He looks so much like Jameson just then, all brooding and grumpy.

"You two look alike," I blurt out, changing the topic.

That draws two dark gazes my way.

"Well, we are brothers," Jameson says, sipping his drink.

"Though I try to deny it," adds Gunnar. "It's hard when you are one of three clones, essentially."

I seize on that topic. "Do you guys have any family photos? I want to know who you look like."

Jameson scowls. "We look like our dad. Except for the eyes... dad had blue eyes. We got our eyes from our mom."

"And yes, Jameson has pictures," Gunnar adds. "He just doesn't like to show them around."

I look to Jameson. "You'd show them to me, wouldn't you?"

"If that's what you want." Jameson looks extremely uncomfortable.

I bite my lip. "I want to know everything that there is to know about you. That means that I want to know about your past. Even the unpleasant parts."

Jameson scoffs. "Alright."

My eyes widen. "I mean it! I want to know it all."

Just then the waiter brings our platters of fajitas and Gunnar's burrito, each one sizzlingly hot and smelling like heaven. Eager for an interruption, Jameson pretends to be very interested in how the fajitas go together.

I make eye contact with Gunnar, who just shrugs and picks up a tortilla from the basket in the middle of the table.

"Where are you guys from? Like, I know that you've lived here for ages, but where are your parents from? And your parents parents?"

Jameson shoves a big tortilla with steak and peppers into his mouth, so that leaves Gunnar to pick up the slack.

"Uhhh... I think our dad was from Montana. Our mom, who knows." Gunnar shrugs.

I take a tortilla, thinking. "Wait, so like... you have no idea if you even have other family? No one has done any research to see if you have any other grandparents or at least cousins floating around out there in the world?"

J and Gunnar shake their heads. I'm a little blown away.

"How is that possible? I mean, when your grandmother died, you didn't even check to see if there was an aunt or an uncle out there?" I ask, growing a little frustrated.

"Nope," Jameson says. He looks at his plate, avoiding eye contact with me.

"She's right, you know," Gunnar says, taking a sip of his drink. "I mean, not that we should have done anything differently. I know that you had a tough enough time as it was, Jameson. But we should do some poking around, see if there are cousins or something."

Jameson seems unconvinced. "I don't know. Maybe."

"You could have a whole bunch of relatives and just not know it," I say. "I'm imagining a whole room full of men that look exactly like you guys do."

"Hmmmph," is all Jameson will say on the subject.

I dig into my food, letting Gunnar and Jameson change the

subject to what bars have opened recently in the area. I definitely won't forget about this though...

I'm already making plans to find a historian who can search what little they know about their past. Maybe I'll do it as a surprise, and then if I find anything worth knowing, I can present it to Jameson as a birthday present or something.

My relationship with Jameson and the fact that we haven't confronted Asher yet is completely lost in the tumult of conversation for now.

22

JAMESON

"What if I get stung again, though?" Emma says, wrinkling her nose.

I'm carrying the surf boards as we hit the beach. It's almost three weeks from the last time I tried to get Emma on a surf board. She tried putting it off yet again, but I wouldn't have it.

I need to surf, and so here we are. I squint at Emma as we walk down the beach in the early morning light. She's wearing a dark blue bikini and carrying her wet suit; with her dark hair and tiny waist, I think she looks like she could easily be a movie star.

I don't tell her that, though. I don't want her to start thinking about her appearance, so I just comfort her fears instead.

"You'll be fine," I say, hefting the boards. "You're going to surf today. I'm going to surf today. And then we'll fuck like two bunny rabbits. Easy peasy."

She pulls a face, but my words seem to have calmed her a little bit. "We'll see about the surfing part. You have way more confidence than I do."

"It's not confidence, it's just knowledge of the facts." We reach a good stopping point, just out of reach of the lapping waves. I set down the boards on the untouched sand. "I know that you can stand and surf. We have been out here too many times for anybody to get in your way, even a jellyfish."

She shudders. "Let's hope so. I would really like to feel what it's like to surf, but I definitely don't need a refresher course on a jellyfish sting."

"Good, cause I left the vinegar in the car this time." I wink at her. "Come on, let's get down to business before the sun gets any higher in the sky."

I pick up one of the surf boards and offer it to her. She takes it, but she lags behind me as I head out into the dark surf with the other board under my arm. I can feel how much she wants to resist, in her heavy steps and her grumpy expression.

"Come on," I chide her gently. I hit the cold morning water, splashing on in it to my knees. "Think of how good it will feel to tell everyone that you can surf."

Emma shoots a skeptical glance at me, but I just hurry further out, sinking into the freezing tide. When I get to my waist, I turn and look at Emma. Emma is almost in up to her chest. I squint, wondering how I almost forgot about our difference in height.

I cast my gaze about, eyeing the distance from the shore. "This is good for your first time."

She looks a little green. "Uh huh..."

"Remember, you just have to get on the board," I say, holding my board by the end. "And then try not to fall."

Emma takes her board by the end, looking behind us. "What am I looking for in a wave?"

"The surf is perfect right now. Pretty much anything you catch that's big enough will do it."

She looks for a minute, then points to a wave that's headed our way. "Like that one?"

"That works. Are you ready?"

She half-nods, distracted by getting on top of her surf board. The wave goes by, breaking right before it reaches us, while Emma is still not ready.

"Crap," she mutters.

"It's okay. There will be another one in just a minute."

She heaves a frustrated sigh, straddling her surfboard. It's kind of cute, how she has no patience for surfing. Outside of law school, she's not used to doing anything that she has to work at. Seeing her actually try and fail is… well, it reminds me that she is human.

"There's another one coming," I point out. I don't even bother to get on my board. This is her time to shine.

The wave comes in, and she looks like she is fiercely concentrating. As the wave picks her up, I see her flounder a little, and then she falls off the board. The wave goes over her head, and I wince.

She comes back up to the surface, spluttering. She's a little baffled. "I fell!"

"I saw," I say, making my way over to her. I scan her for injuries. "You okay?"

"Yeah. Only my pride was hurt," she quips. "I'm going to paddle out a bit and try again."

I grin. "Atta girl."

I drift in her wake as she goes out a little further, then gets astride the board again. As I watch, she waits for a wave to swell beneath her. It begins to propel her toward the shore, and she rises on the surf board.

I hold my breath as Emma makes it to her feet, whooshing past me. As she goes, she shouts to me. "I'm doing it! Jameson, I'm really surfing!"

She looks at me instead of looking at the water before her. She wipes out big time, falling sideways off of her board. I'm already swimming towards her when she resurfaces, her hair plastered to the side of her skull.

Although she just fell, she's all smiles when she sees me.

"I did it! I am terrible at surfing, but at least I did it." She grins at me. I close in for a hug, picking her up.

Her arms settle around my neck, and she looks up at me.

"Ready to go again?" I ask.

"You know what? I think I'm good," she says with a shrug. "I would honestly rather sit and watch you surf while I have a drink."

I chuckle. "That's it, huh? You just had to make sure you could do it?"

"Precisely." She squints up at me. "I feel fulfilled."

"Well, alright then," I say. "Do you mind if I surf for a little while?"

"Definitely not." She releases her grip on my shoulders, stepping back. "I'll be on the beach, doing a little yoga."

As I watch, she turns and heads for the shore, her hips swaying. I shake my head and make my way further out into the dark blue ocean.

23

JAMESON

Later, after we've fucked ourselves senseless, I come back into the bedroom with a big Nalgene full of water. Emma is sprawled out on her stomach, completely naked.

I don't know what it says about me, but the fact that I can see faint traces of my handprints on her ass turns me the fuck on. She turns her head to the side, her eyes following me into the room. I really did give her a good workout, and I'm not even done.

I try to ignore my hardening cock and focus on caring for Emma right now.

"Drink," I order her, putting the Nalgene on the bed in front of her face.

She lifts her eyebrows, but rolls onto her side and picks up the Nalgene bottom. Unscrewing the cap, she chugs a quarter of the water. I watch as a couple of drops escape to dribble down the side of her mouth, one tracing its way down her throat.

I swallow at that. If my erection was tentative before, it's definitely not now. She may be my girlfriend, but that doesn't begin to stop me from constantly eye fucking her. The thirst is real, and I don't think that's going to change anytime soon.

Emma sets the Nalgene bottle down and looks at me. "Happy?"

"Nah. Between the day at the beach and a couple hours in here, I think you need way more of that. There is no way you're not dehydrated by now."

"And you're not?" She scowls, but she takes another swig.

"You're right," I say, sitting on the bed. "Pass it over here."

She does, and I gulp down half of the contents in one go. I make a satisfied sound and pass it back. She sighs and sits up, taking the bottle. I stare at her tits, where I see my handiwork present too, right around her nipples.

She sips from the water bottle, not commenting on the fact that I'm just ogling her openly. I let my eyes unfocus for a second, and I let my mind imagine a day when she might not be as willing to let me ravage her over and over again. It's in the future, for sure… but it's not that distant, when I really think about it.

"Where do you see us going, as a couple?"

The words are out of my mouth before I've even considered the thought myself. Emma freezes for a second, mid-mouthful of water. She swallows it slowly.

"Ummm…" she says, scrunching her face up. "Do you mean like… generally? What do you mean?"

That's a good question. What exactly am I looking for? I feel like such a woman, having all of these feelings.

"I don't know. I just… I took you house shopping, because it seemed like the thing to do. And we found a great space that I can see us growing older together in. But… what else are you looking for, future-wise?"

She nods slowly. I can see the gears turning. "Future wise? I guess… I mean, I want a marriage. I want kids. I want to work as a lawyer. Other than that, I don't really have anything specifically planned."

"Hmm," I say, nodding. "Good answer."

"What about you? You've lived longer than I have," she teases. "Surely you've got a plan in place?"

"Well, yeah. I'm sort of your opposite. I have the career planned out, and I've always sort of dreamed of having that beach house, in the back of my mind. But until a couple of months ago, I wasn't even sure that I would end up with anybody." I pause for a second. "I used to be like, I'll just get married on the sly, no one even has to know."

She laughs. "I like that about you."

I roll my eyes, my face beginning to burn. "Yeah, well. You ruined it. Now I'm like, when is too soon to propose? When can we... you know... have kids? All that kind of shit."

Her perfectly pink mouth goes round in surprise. "You're thinking... I mean... I didn't realize you really meant long term. I just thought that I was being silly."

My ears burning bright red, I shake my head. "Nope. Or at least, if you're being silly, then I am too. But... you know I love you. And I don't exactly say that a lot."

Her eyes turn glossy with unshed tears. "I know. You have to know that I love you too. Like, so much that it's crazy."

I move forward, leaning down to kiss her on the lips. A voice inside my head demands that I grab her tits, that I feel her ass jiggle as I smack it. But I have to learn to quiet that voice, every once in a while.

My lips curve upwards, and I break the kiss. She looks at me, thinking what I'm thinking.

"That was very restrained," she says, patting me appreciatively. "I like that you're really very serious about me finishing my water."

"Hydration is important," I say with a shrug. "Tomorrow, I'll go by the store and stock up on some gatorade and coconut water."

"How very thoughtful of you." She drinks some more water.

Silence falls between us, weirdly comfortable. I lie down with my head in her lap, and she allows it. I watch her face, thinking how lucky I am that her eyes and mouth are so expressive. I can tell when she has a thought, because she looks at me, as if she's not sure she should share it.

"What?" I ask. Obviously I catch her off guard, and she blushes.

"Umm." She screws the lid back on the water bottle, and sets it aside. Leaning back a little, she combs her fingers through my hair. "Remember when you broke up with me?"

I wince at her words. "Yeah, of course. I was being a dumbass."

"I was pretty upset," she says, looking away from me.

"Yes. I remember it. I'm sorry for the pain I caused." I take her other hand, lacing our fingers together. I feel guilty as sin as I look at how small and delicate her fingers are next to mine.

"I thought…" She pauses, stumbling over her words. When she says the next bit, it all comes out rushed. "I thought I was pregnant. And I thought you had left me. And I just… I freaked out."

My fingers freeze. I'm alarmed, more than I have the right to be. "Wait, I thought you were on the pill."

"An IUD," she corrects gently. "And I am. But I thought… just for a minute, I thought I might be carrying your baby."

"Yeah?" I ask, because that's all I know to say. My mouth is suddenly really dry.

"I don't know. I don't know why I'm telling you about it, honestly. I guess I just felt… like relieved, at the same time as sort of sad?" she admits.

I squeeze her fingers. "I would have done the right thing, you know."

"Yeah, but… I'm glad that it didn't go down like that. I think that I would've always had a nagging voice in the back of my head that wondered if you would've come back to me or not without the pregnancy. This way, I just know."

She uncaps the water bottle, drinking almost all of it. I take it from her, finish it, and roll to my feet.

"I'm glad it worked out like it did. And don't think for a hot second that it will at all deter me from enjoying your body." I lean down for a kiss. She didn't have to tell me that... she just felt comfortable enough to confide it. I don't want to discourage that, at all. I pull away from the kiss, my eyes twinkling. "I think we're going to need another one of these, just to keep going."

She arches a brow. "Are we going to keep going?"

"Fuck yes we are," I tell her. "If I have my way, we'll be doing this when we're eighty."

She smiles widely. I grin down at her, then carry the water bottle toward the hallway.

24

EMMA

I look at the time, sighing. I'm standing in my kitchen, making tea and talking to my mother over speakerphone. My mother is rattling on about how no one in her book club even reads the books.

I'm hardly listening though. My head is with Jameson, focusing on where he is right now. At this moment, he's probably sitting in a sterile-looking classroom, taking the GED. He's been stressed about it for the last few days, even though he didn't say so.

I know that he's smart and capable no matter what, but I need him to pass this so that he knows it too. I dunk the teabag in my mug, sighing again.

"Emmaline, are you even listening?" my mother scolds. Her voice coming through the speakerphone is tinny.

I straighten my spine. "Uh, yeah. Definitely."

"I just asked you whether or not you're coming to the Labor Day party that your father and I throw every year. I think there will be a lot of eligible guys there…"

I clear my throat. "We talked about this, mother. You aren't allowed to set me up with your friend's kids anymore. Not after what happened last time."

She scoffs. "Rich was just a one time thing. I promise you, there are a ton of other eligible men."

"I'm dating someone else, as I have repeatedly told you." I let a note of frustration creep into my voice.

"Darling, I just want to see you find the person you'll eventually marry. I'm sure that whoever you're seeing is perfectly nice, but I assume he is lacking in the pedigree department. And pedigree counts more and more as you get older."

I roll my eyes. "You have no idea what kind of person I'm dating. You don't even know what I *like*."

"Emmaline," my mother sighs. "If he was really that great, you would have brought him to meet me already. That's a fact."

I'm taken aback by her words. Is that true? Have I been hiding Jameson from her intentionally?

"I'm just… not ready to introduce *you* into *his* life yet. You're a handful, mother." That statement is mostly true, too.

My mother's voice grows snippy. "Oh, please. You're just worried that your new beau won't live up to my standards. You think that you can just live in your happy little bubble, and not interact with the people who really matter in your life."

"What? I'm sorry, but I fail to see what exactly you are saying."

"I'm saying that the fact that your father and I don't talk to your big brother might have led you to believe that you are just going to live your life any kind of way, without repercussions. But we both know that when it comes down to what matters — when it's about money — you don't where you get your bread buttered. I didn't raise you to be a stupid girl, Emmaline."

I am absolutely floored by her words. I'm glad that she's just on the phone and not here in person, because I'm sure I have the bitterest look on my face.

"I should really go," I say, trying to keep the rage out of my voice. "It is always nice to talk to you, mother."

"Emmaline—"

I disconnect the call, my fingers shaking. I can't believe her, I really can't. I've really never thought about how dependent I am on my family's money before, but my mother made it perfectly clear that she has no problem using money as a chain to bind me to the family's side.

My mother seems to assume that I will automatically bend to her will as soon as she cracks the whip, even if that means dating someone she approves of.

What the hell am I supposed to do with that? I have to do something soon to let her know that I'm not going to be cowed... I just don't know what exactly to do.

My phone vibrates. When I check it, there's a message from Jameson.

Done and on my way to you, it says.

I blow out a shaky breath. I dump out my now-cold tea in the kitchen sink, focusing on getting myself dressed and ready. After all, Jameson is going to come home, and I want to celebrate with him. It'll probably be awhile before he gets his test results, but today was a really big deal for him.

I put on a white cotton sundress, figuring it isn't even going to be on my body for long. I have a ton of thoughts swirling around inside my head right now, but I need to put them aside. Right now, I just need to focus on supporting my boyfriend.

When I hear the front door open, I pop my head out of my bedroom. Jameson is grinning from ear to ear, pouncing on me. I squeal as he picks me up for a kiss, spinning me around. His kiss is sweet and slow and heated.

When I pull back, I look up at him with a smile. "Are you excited about the GED being over, then?"

He kisses me again, nodding. "That's one of the things I'm excited about."

I giggle as he carries me backward into the bedroom, collapsing on the bed, cradling me in his arms. "Is there something else to celebrate?"

Jameson kisses my collarbone, working his way down to my cleavage. At the same time, he shifts his weight onto the bed and slides his hand up my outer thigh. "Yep. Two things. Well... three."

"And what are those three things, exactly?"

I bite my lip as his hand continues its exploration up my skirt, toying with the hem of my panties. He pulls his head back to look at me.

"One, you're wearing this dress, and looking like you do. If that's not a reason, I don't even know what would be."

I smirk. "Yeah, all right. What else?"

"Well..." he says, reaching over to brush my hair back from my neck. He places a chaste kiss there, but his scruffy beard scrapes against my skin lightly, making me shiver. "I made an offer on the house yesterday morning... and today, I heard back."

I sit up, suddenly alert. "Wait, you made an offer? What did they say?"

Jameson's face splits into a grin. "They said yes. You are looking at a home owner."

I fling my arms around his neck and hug him, smiling so hard that it practically hurts. "Oh my god! That's amazing news!!"

"Yep. We have a standard thirty day closing period, and then I get the keys. So I'm pretty excited about that."

"Uh, *yeah*," I say, pulling back to look at him. "You're going to be a home owner!! Congratulations!!"

He smiles a little sheepishly. "Thanks. Taking the GED, buying a house... it feels like the direction I want my life to be going."

"I am so, so proud of you." I beam at him. "Really, so proud. I'll get to introduce you to people as my boyfriend AND a home owner. 'I'm sorry, have you met my homeowning boyfriend?. He's great.'"

"Only if I get to call you my law school girlfriend. You know, to make things even." Jameson slips a finger under the strap of my dress, tugging it down my shoulder.

"Mmmm," I murmur. "Wait, but isn't there a third thing you should be celebrating? Whatever that news is, I can't wait to hear it."

He looks at me mischievously. "You're going to have to wait a little while. But I promise, it will be worth it."

The look in his eyes promises more than that. I blush, which feels utterly ridiculous after all that we've been through together.

"Are you sure?" I ask, linking my fingers with his. "I mean, you don't have to wait on my account, is what I'm saying."

He grins. "I promise, it will be worth it when I finally tell you."

Before I can say another word, he strips my panties off of my legs and claims my mouth with his.

25

EMMA

I lean into the kiss before I am even certain what is happening. His hand cups my chin and controls my head. With my head lifted towards him, his lips are on mine. I can taste nothing but the flavor of him, clean and masculine and raw.

When his tongue slips between my lips, I let out a moan, meeting it with my own. My back arches, my chest press up against him. He explores the stretch of silky skin at my hip, and slowly moves lower, lower. He drags out every moment, an exquisite torture.

I slide his jacket off his shoulders hungrily while he grabs my thigh and drapes it across his lap, leaving me exposed. His hand travels up toward my center, kneading and squeezing my thigh as he goes.

When his fingers brush my core, he finds me already wet.

"This?" he says, his voice gone to gravel. He teases my crevice again with the lightest of touches. "This is mine."

I can do nothing but gasp and nod.

He grins and squeezes my ass as he pulls me on top of his lap. As I straddle him, I can feel his cock between my legs, wrapped in his jeans. I'm already wet, but can't help grinding against him.

Even through his pants, I feel his heated weight, and I'm ready for him to tear off the rest of our clothes and fuck me right this second.

It's never that easy or fast with Jameson, though. He likes to take it slow, to tease and torture me.

His mouth moves from my lips to my jaw and travels to my neck. The light cotton of the dresses neckline stops him, and he growls. With one hand—the other still firmly on my backside—he pulls the straps down my arms, baring me to the waist. It falls quickly around my waist and exposes my breasts.

A part of me feels suddenly shy, even though this was far from our first time together. Jameson smirks at my shyness. "You know that you are probably the most beautiful girl I've ever seen?"

His hand snakes below the folds of the dress, which is now solely held against my body at the waist. He holds me up above him so my nipples meet his mouth. I feel his fingers digging into my ass cheeks, dangerously close to my pussy, as the warmth of his mouth consumes one nipple, and the other.

I whimper as I feel my nipples harden against his tongue. I want desperately to be lower, to be able to rub myself against his cock again, but he keeps me firmly poised inches above his lap.

I squirm, and his hands that clutch my bare ass shift closer to my center. His fingers slowly, slowly spread me apart. The ache of emptiness is unbearable.

"Fuck, you're wet," he tells me between sucks on my nipples.

"Stop teasing me," I say, frustrated.

"Is this what you want?" he asks as he lowers me back down.

Instead of letting me go completely, he slid a finger inside my pussy and pushes his thumb against my clit. I shudder at the surprise of it—and the pleasure of having some part of him inside me.

I can't bring myself to reply, but I move against his hand eagerly. His hands are deft, with practiced flicks against my G-spot and just enough pressure on my clit to get me halfway to orgasm. But no closer.

I kiss him deeply, eyes squeezing shut. All I want is to come.

"Slow down," he tells me. "Enjoy the ride, princess."

There is a part of me that thought maybe he'll just stop. Maybe it is all just a game, a power trip. I ride his hand harder, lifting my head, and offer my breasts to his lips again. He spanks me once once on my ass, hard.

"I said slow down," he growls.

The slap surprises me, but even as the sting fades and I feel my ass turning red, I also feel a new gush of wetness between my thighs. My pussy is on fire, and I need him like I've never needed him before.

He slips his finger out of my pussy and flips me onto my back. The coolness of the bed is a shock to my skin. He kneels and spreads my legs wide.

"You really are ravishing," he tells me. "And I'm about to ravage you."

I smile and let my head fall back as he kisses his way down my thighs. When he reaches my mound, he kisses his way across it, trailing his tongue against my sweat-slicked skin. He comes so close to tasting me, really tasting my pussy, and yet he pulls back.

I shake my head back and forth, ready to burst.

"Fuck! Jameson, come on!" I cry, pounding my fists.

"What do you want?" he asks me, smirking.

"Jameson, *please*," I say, arching my back as far as I can.

"You're going to have to tell me," he says tauntingly.

I bite my lip just as he blows lightly on my clit.

"I want you to eat my... eat my pussy," I say, going red as I say the words.

"Good girl." He grins before he lowers himself to my flesh.

His tongue runs across my clit, firm and slow, before it dips down into the deepest of my folds. I cry out and dig my fingers into his hair to hold him closer to me.

"Oh god. Oh, Jameson!!" As he works his tongue faster, I can't stop calling out his name. When he slid a finger into me again, I reach for my breasts and pinch my nipples.

I don't want to come, not like this. Not without giving him a taste of his own medicine.

"I want to taste you," I say, breathless. He pulls his finger from my body and leaves a flutter of kisses on my clit.

"What about you? Don't you want to come?" he asks, even as he unbuckles his trousers and I slip completely out of the dress.

"I want you to feel good first... and then I want us to come together," I say.

When he unzips and shows me his cock, I bite my lip. I know I've seen it all before, but his cock is so perfect, so thick and long, so perfectly pink. That ache that throbbing deep inside of me doesn't have a chance of stopping.

I reach for him, but he stops me.

"How about a little dessert?" he asks, and pulls a can of whipped cream up from its hiding place on the floor.

"Yesss," I say, my excitement growing by the moment.

He spread the cool sticky slickness across my breasts—and along his shaft. He straddles my chest and takes my hands in his.

"Press your tits together," he encourages me. "They're already so fucking hot, you know that?"

I blush, eagerly pressing my breasts together. As soon as I do, he slides his cock between my breasts, the tip reaching to my mouth. I lick and suck at him like a starving creature. The heat of his length between my breasts and the sweetness of the cream blended with his own taste in a way that is intoxicating.

He keeps one hand loosely on my head and caresses my cheek while he watches me take him deeper and deeper into my mouth. He rises up, brushes my hands away from my breasts, leans down and kisses me. He laps up every last bit of the cream, from my lips to my swollen nipples.

"Every part of you tastes so good," he whispers. I want to tell him the same, but my jaw aches and my lips are numb from sucking on just the couple of inches he gave me.

Standing up, he stretches briefly.

I laugh. "What are you doing?"

"I want to fuck you properly," he says. "I gotta stay flexible, you know?"

His grin is infectious. I grin right back at him, crooking a finger. "Come here."

Jameson climbs on the bed, looming over me.

When he penetrates me, I am shockingly tight. It feels so fucking good. I feel every single inch of him as he thrusts his long, proud cock inside my body.

"Are you okay?" he asks me.

"Yes, yes," I breathe into his ear. "Please... I want you to fuck me. *Please*, Jameson."

He buries his face in my neck and breathes me in. He takes his time, sliding in and out of my pussy oh so slowly.

When he teases me, lingering with barely his tip inside me, I struggle and demand that he go deep. Every time he slides against my g-spot, I scratch at his back and call out his name.

"Jameson, yes! Oh, please don't stop."

I am so wet it is almost unbelievable. He kisses me, slowing even though I just told him not to.

"Not so fast. I want you to slow it all down. Get on top," he tells me. "I want to watch you."

I bite my lip, and he switches our positions. On his back, he watches me straddle him. My hair has come undone and hangs in knotted waves over my breasts. He reaches up, pushes the hair aside, and pulls my nipples. I look down and grasp his cock to bring him to my opening.

He moves his hands to my hips.

"Slowly," he tells me. "Remember what I said."

I let my weight fall onto him, but he holds me up. I blush again. He seems to want to watch me take his cock into my pussy.

"Please," I whisper when he is halfway in. He pulls me down, hard, onto him. I throw my head back and call out.

My nails dig into his chest and he clutches my ass as I ride him. It's perfect, the two of us moving as one, our breathing harsh. My breasts bounce wildly. Every part of his skin feels like silk underneath my fingertips. My wetness is so intense it drips down between his thighs.

My eyes close tight and I grind hard against him.

"Look at me," he tells me.

I open my eyes and he can tell I am close.

"I love you. I love you so fucking much," he says, his dark eyes intense on mine.

"I love you too," I whisper, my breath coming in gasps.

He pushes himself up and wraps my legs around his back. From here, he is in complete control — and my nipples are once again aligned with his face.

He lifts me and lowers me onto his cock, while he covers my chest in marks that I knew would darken to hickeys by the next day. I score his back with my nails, marking him in my own way.

My legs are locked around him, his lap soaking with my juices.

"I—" I gasp out. "I'm going to come..."

He can feel my orgasm start to wash over me as the heat of my insides clench. It is enough to push him over the edge and he comes with me. When he explodes inside of me, I scream out loud.

"Fuck! Emma, fuck," he whispers.

I shudder against him as I ride out the last of my orgasm. He kisses my neck gently and makes his way to my lips.

Jameson lies beside me, lining our bodies up and holding me close as I struggle for breath. He's breathing hard too, but he kisses my neck, my shoulder, the curve of my breast. Each kiss is a burning brand, causing a shudder to ripple across my exhaust body.

I want to beg him to stop, but I also want to have him again, right now. There's something about him that just makes me insatiable. He looks up at me, then presses a kiss to my lips.

"Fuck," he says softly, making eye contact with me.

I can't help but laugh a little. "What?"

"Just... I was going to do this later, after I had ask your father..." He sits up, searching the floor. "I can't wait, though. Not with you."

I raise myself up on one elbow, cocking my head. "What are you talking about?"

Jameson pulls on his boxer briefs and keeps searching, though I can't for the life of me figure out what he's looking for. He finally finds his discarded pants, fishing something out.

When he turns to me, he says, "You're going to want to be sitting up for this."

I sit up, grabbing a pillow to put in my lap. "I'm sorry, for what exactly?"

Then Jameson drops to one knee, a solemn look on his face. I'm completely confused for a second, until he flashes me a little black velvet ring box. My hands fly to my mouth, and I look at him.

He opens the box with a snap. Inside a perfect diamond glints, an emerald cut set with baguette diamonds beside it. I can't even process it.

"What??" I whisper. "Oh, Jameson..."

He shushes me. "Shh, let me do this properly. Emma Alderisi, you've known for years what I've only recently come to realize. We were meant to be together. I know it in my soul. You're smart, and kind, and you always have my back. Will you also take my last name?"

I'm so astonish, my mouth just hangs agape. Jameson gives me a smile, my favorite one that is part dimple, and asks the question.

"Emma, will you marry me?"

My eyes well up, and I have to fan myself as I nod. "Yes. Oh my god, yes."

He pulls the ring from the box, motioning for me to give him my hand. I do, tears beginning to roll down my face. He is all smiles as he puts the ring on me.

I launch myself off the bed and into his arms, knocking him over on the floor. He laughs out loud, a truly delighted sound. Then he can't do anything but grin as I cover his entire face with kisses.

"I love you," I say, feverishly kissing his lips.

He tries to say something back, probably *I love you too*. But I'm not listening, not even one little bit. This man, this wonderful man who just makes my entire world complete, has many more kisses to receive.

And I happen to be the lucky girl that gets to deliver them.

26

EMMA

I sigh, turning over to look at Jameson. It's really late, or maybe really early. The street lamp outside casts its glow onto his face, the blinds on the window causing it to fall in little stripes.

The light catches my engagement ring as I turn, throwing rainbows on the bed. I bite my lip. I'm still not used to the idea of belonging to him, or of wearing his ring.

I scrunch up my face at the ring. Not that anyone could possibly make me take it off or anything... but I have to wonder what Asher will say. Or my parents.

Or anyone, really. I mean, I haven't tried to not tell anyone. It's just been a challenge to leave the bedroom for the last couple of days. Every time I get up, Jameson pulls me back in with a lure that works every time.

I blush, recalling all the hours of hot, sweaty sex. And it's Jameson — realistically, the sex could just be okay and I would still be thrilled that he finally chose me. The fact that he put a ring on it was just...

I don't even have the words to explain to anyone else how fucking elated I am. If you asked thirteen year old me how she saw things playing out between Jameson and me, I really don't think she would've come up with this as a scenario. That's how in awe I am of it.

But I'm still worried. Worried about how Asher will react, that it will go beyond just a lot of yelling. Worried that my parents will scare Jameson off somehow.

I sigh again, and Jameson cracks open an eye. "Are you sighing passive aggressively at me, or actually worried about something?"

I turn pink. "Ohhh, sorry! No, I'm not being passive aggressive. I didn't realize you could hear me."

He opens his eyes a little further, moving to sit up. "What's on your mind, oh wife to be?"

"You won't like it."

"I'm already awake at four in the morning. Obviously it's enough to keep you tossing and turning even after hours of sex. So how about you just tell me what it is?"

I look down at the bed, tracing a figure eight in the sheets. "I uh... I'm more than a little worried about what Asher will do when he finds out. I mean... I just don't want anything else to come between us, you know?"

His brow puckers. "You're worried that he will do something that makes me not want to marry you?"

"No. Well, maybe. I don't know." I refuse to look up at him, even though I can feel his eyes on my face.

He scoots closer, using two fingers to lift up my chin. I stare at his black-brown eyes, so perplexed with me at this moment.

"What would he do? I can't imagine a single thing that Asher could do that would change how I feel in here." He taps his chest. "I know that I've let you down before—"

My eyes well up and my lip starts to tremble. "You guys have so much history together... how can I hope to overcome that?"

He smiles. "You have overcome it. That's what you don't understand, I think. I'm in it, Em. I am in this, with you, forever. End of story."

"Jameson—" I whisper, a tear breaking free to track down my

face. I love what he is saying, but I'm afraid at the same time. "Don't say it. I don't think you mean it, not all the way. What if—what if my parents are horrible and nasty to you? What if Asher won't ever talk to you again? What if—"

I break off, stifling a sob. Jameson wipes away the tear from my face and ever so gently kisses my lips.

"Shh," he says, comforting me. "I know I hurt you. And I wish like hell every single day that I hadn't. I just... I realized that you were right."

I'm actively just sobbing in his arms now. When I speak, it comes out all strangled, and broken up by hiccups. "I.. I was?"

He pushes my hair back off my forehead. "Yes. You asked when I was going to be done owing Asher. It didn't quite sink in then, but later... I realized that you were right. I get the feeling that you're almost always right about things like that."

I snuggle in closer to his neck, getting a big lungful of his scent. I try to calm down as much as possible. "Oh."

He kisses the crown of my head. I try to reconcile what Jameson has just told me with the turmoil that's been in my head recently, but it's tough. I burrow even deeper against Jameson's neck, my eyelids growing heavy.

I must have drifted off, because the next thing I know, I'm blinking against the midmorning light. Jameson is nowhere to be seen, but when I put my hand out, his spot in the bed is still warm. I sit up, a little disoriented.

Jameson comes in with two mugs of coffee. He's dressed in nothing but his boxer briefs, and for a second I wonder how in the hell I got so lucky.

I mean, this is the man that is supposedly going to bring me coffee every day for the rest of my frigging life. It doesn't seem true, but somehow it's happening to me anyway.

"Here," he says, handing me a mug. He sits down beside me, and I look at my coffee. It's steaming, the color of thick mud, and it smells friggin amazing.

"You're up and awake," I say, eyeing him suspiciously. "What's going on?"

He gives me a crooked smile. "I just woke up before you. And I was thinking about what you said last night, that you were still stressed about telling your brother."

I nod, blowing on my coffee before taking a too-hot sip.

"Yep. It is literally keeping me awake at night."

He takes a deep breath. "Well, I think we should just tell him. Get it over with."

I glance at him, a little worried. "You do? I mean, I didn't mean to infect you with my worries."

Jameson splays his big hand out over my knee. "Your worries are my worries now. And besides, hiding our relationship from him is childish."

I suck my lower lip in between my teeth, thinking it over. "I mean, you are absolutely right. But it just seems so hard. Like… I would just rather avoid it, if at all possible. Just bury myself under the covers with you forever, and never come out."

His dimple flashes. "Yeah, I'd prefer that too. But that's not a real option, so… it's better if we just get it out of the way. I mean, assuming you're going to come with me. I don't know if I would, if I were you."

I roll my eyes. "Of course I'm going to come with you. I think that it will lessen your chances of brawling on the street, anyway."

"Hey, the only time I've really done that was for you," he says, but I can tell he's joking.

"Have I told you thank you yet?" I ask, moving forward just enough to kiss his shoulder. "I appreciate it."

"Remember that feeling, because I think we should go to Cure right now. I texted Asher to find out where he will be, and he's apparently doing inventory over there as we speak."

I blanch, even though I know that this is something that we have to do. I sigh. "Thus the coffee?"

"Yep." He pats my knee. "Then afterward, we'll do something fun. Like putt putt or go karts or something."

I give him a look. "Can there be ice cream involved?"

He grins. "Every flavor you could possibly want."

"Uuuugh, okay. I'll get dressed." I swat him on his butt as he gets up, taking just one more second to appreciate how amazingly hot he is.

I drink my coffee as I get ready in a blue sundress. I'm nervous beyond words as Jameson drives us both over to Cure, staring off into the distance. I can't help the thoughts that are filling my mind.

What will Asher say? It seems unlikely that he will surprise me by simply being okay with our newfound relationship.

I glance at Jameson. I'm honestly more worried about the effect that Asher's words will have on him. Actually, worried is the wrong word. It's more of a distinct note of dread.

Jameson says all the right things, about how he's in this relationship for the long haul. But what if his heart isn't in it after we confront Asher?

Jameson parks the back lot, and I take a deep breath. He leads me through the alley and up onto the patio, toward the shaded glass doors. He uses his keys and pulls the door open, waiting for me to go first.

I step in, blinking against the bright overhead lights. It's a Saturday morning, so the bar is completely empty. There are cases and cases of liquor stacked on the bar, out of place.

"Hello?" I call out, trying not to let my voice shake.

Jameson gives my arm a squeeze, pushing past me. Asher's blond head pokes out of the back office, frowning. "Jameson, hi. What are you doing here, Em?"

I clear my throat, trailing after Jameson. "I'm here with Jameson."

Asher looks between Jameson and me, confused. "Okay?"

"We have something to tell you," Jameson says, his expression unreadable. He seems already hardened, in preparation for whatever is about to go down.

Jameson reaches a hand over to me. I take it like it's a lifeline and I'm drowning in the big, black sea.

"You—" Asher steps out of the office, looking pointedly at our clasped hands. "No. No way."

He looks to Jameson, his expression demanding an explanation.

"We're dating," I blurt out. Jameson gives me a little side eye.

"Actually, we're engaged," Jameson says.

Asher seems stunned for a moment, his fists clenching. "Are you— is this a joke? This isn't funny."

"It's very real," I say, holding out my left hand. "Jameson made it official a few days ago."

"Jameson— Emma— what the fuck??" Asher says, anger tingeing his voice. "How could this happen?"

I step closer to Jameson, my cheeks burning. "You had to know how I've felt about about Jameson for all these years."

Jameson cuts in. "I'm sorry that we broke your rule, but I'm not sorry about finding happiness with Emma. She makes me happy, Asher."

For a second, I think that Asher is just totally going to lose his shit. Every muscle in his body is clenched tightly, and he's looking at Jameson like Jameson just betrayed him. When he speaks, it's with a barely contained rage.

"I don't even know you anymore," he says to Jameson. "I've felt like that for a while—"

"You mean ever since you got back together with Evie and didn't need me anymore?" Jameson growls.

If looks could kill, the one passing between Jameson and Asher right now would be deadly, without a doubt.

Asher looks at me pointedly. "Our parents will never allow this."

That is low, even for him. Asher doesn't even speak to our

parents anymore! "Really? That's your tactic here? To invoke what our parents may do?"

"I'll tell them," Asher threatens. "I'll tell them you're actually so confused as to think that you are marrying him. You know that he's— he's not like us!"

"What, rich and privileged?" I spit back. "Jameson's doing just fine by my book."

Asher levels a look at Jameson. "You're basically guaranteeing that Cure doesn't last another year. You know that, right?"

Jameson glares at him. "Who do you think made this place so great? It wasn't you, that's for damn sure. If Cure goes under, I will just start another business, one that isn't tied to your dirty family money."

"That's it! You two are fucking making me crazy!" Asher yells, bursting past us both, headed for the front door. "Good fucking luck not running this place into the ground."

As I watch, Asher pushes open the door, and slams out of the building. I look to Jameson, my eyes a little wide.

"Did he just quit the business?" I ask.

"Yeah, I think so," Jameson says. "And… I hate to say this, but you had better call your parents. Tell them that you want to meet them as soon as you can. I think it's better if we tell them about our engagement, rather than just hearing Asher spouting off about it."

Oh god. That's a lot of people that will be angry at me, in such a short time. I feel like there is a huge lump in my throat.

A deep breath in, and a deep breath out. I bite my lip, holding onto Jameson's arm. "Are you okay?"

Jameson looks down at the ground. "Yeah. I mean, it sucks that my best friend acted like that, but… I'm doing okay."

"I'm sorry that Asher was an ass. You don't deserve that, at all." I lace my fingers with his, giving his hand a squeeze.

Jameson shrugs. "Honestly, it went better than I expected. I thought he was going to take a swing at me and say horrible stuff. Instead, he just said horrible stuff."

I give him a faint smile. "I know. Still… I'm sorry, anyway."

He leans down for a kiss, slow and hot, making my toes curl up. "I still get you. Asher will come around eventually, or maybe not. But either way, I still get the girl. I'm the winner here, I think."

I beam at him, my heart swelling. "I really love you."

"And I love you. I keep telling you, I'm in this for the long run."

And for the first time, standing in Cure, I let myself really, actually believe him.

27

JAMESON

I straighten my tie again as we walk into Lyre, the fancy restaurant that Emma's parents chose to meet her at. As Emma gives her name at the hostess stand and the hostess ushers us onward through the restaurant, I can't help my racing heart.

I put my hand onto Emma's lower back as we walk, unnerved. She's wearing a lemon yellow dress, and I'm wearing a full suit. I'm fucking sweating, and not just because it's hot outside. I won't show it outside, but in my head, I'm all but shaking with my fear.

I know how this will probably go. In all likelihood, her parents will see us together, see us touching, and get angry. They'll know who I am; after all, they kicked me and my brothers out of squatting on their property no less then four separate times.

They'll know that I come from nothing. They'll know that I'm not good enough for Emma, and that my childhood poverty is only one of the reasons that makes me unworthy.

And if Asher had anything to say about it, I'm sure that his parents already know that their family money financed Cure. So even the bar, which is definitely *my* baby, wont really help me out here.

I am second guessing myself, second guessing everything I am, on this walk through the tables. Everything sort of blurs as we walk: the white linen tablecloths, the patrons talking, the faint chime of glassware and tableware being moved around. It only occurs to me when we see Emma's parents that I've not only agreed to live out my worst nightmare, but I encouraged it.

What the fuck was I thinking?

But then there they are, the Alderisis. Albert is in his late fifties, tall and heavy and silver at the temples. Nancy is a few years younger, and thin as a dagger in her pink dress. My mouth goes dry, my expression hardens.

I see them spot me. I see her father take in the way I'm touching her back. It takes them both a second to place me, but when they do her father turns red and her mother's nostrils flare.

I know that I'm a grown ass man, but in that moment, I'm also a scared little boy. I'm praying that they don't kick my family out of our temporary home.

Emma stands up a little straighter as we approach. Albert throws his linen napkin on the table and starts to stand up. Emma forestalls him with a gesture.

"You both remember Jameson, don't you?" she says.

I slide my glance to her, impressed by how ice cold her tone has become. She primly presses her lips together for a second, waiting for them to speak. Her parents just glower at the two of us.

"Emmaline..." her mother says, her voice high pitched. "This is inappropriate. We should talk about this privately, just the three of us."

"You are fooling no one, young man," her father says to me. "I don't know what you think you're doing here with my little girl-"

"Talk to me!" Emma says, loudly enough to make the couple

seated at the next table stare. "If you have something to say to Jameson, you can address it to me. There's no reason to drag him into the dirt."

"Emma—" her father says, standing up. "I swear to god, you need to quit playing games, here."

Emma's jaw juts out, and she cocks her hip. "My relationship with Jameson is serious. Dead serious. As in, I'm wearing his ring, kind of serious."

Nancy gasps, her hand flying over her mouth. Albert begins to sweat, his veins in his forehead popping out.

"You listen to me, little girl," he sneers.

"No!" Emma says.

"Em—" I try to interject, but she shoots me a look that makes me shut up.

"Listen to me," she says, taking my hand. "You already lost Asher over trying to dictate who he could and could not marry. Anything you do to punish me? It will only drive me away, just like it did with him. Are you ready to do that?"

Her father loses his shit. "You foolish little—"

"Stop!" Nancy shouts, drawing the eyes of everyone in the restaurant. She stands up, folding her napkin and putting it on the table. "Would you two like to sit?"

"Like hell they're going to sit!" Albert growls.

Nancy looks at him, and there is something that passes between them, some sort of argument. After a second, it's clear that Nancy wins. She turns to us with a frosty smile.

"You'll sit, won't you?" She motions to the two unoccupied chairs at the table.

I blink, confused. Albert is still furious and red, but he just sits back down, yanking his napkin off the table. Nancy continues to look at us questioningly.

I look to Emma, who looks like she's just won some kind of war. "Are we going to sit?"

"Yes, I think so." Her lips curve upwards in a smile.

I pull out her chair for her, and then sit beside her. Nancy sits too, tucking her napkin back on her lap.

"Champagne?" Nancy asks, her expression unreadable. "One should toast good news, like that of being engaged. Right?"

"Right," Emma says lightly. "We definitely should."

Her mother snaps her fingers, calling for the waiter. When Emma picks her menu up, I can see her trembling. I stare for a second, then reach out and cover her shaking fingers with my own.

Emma looks at me. For a moment, I can see everything she has been hiding since the moment we walked into this restaurant. The fear, the pain, the anxiety, all pent up.

She was just as nervous as I was, just as afraid. She just spoke up anyway.

I kiss her knuckles, unbelievably glad that I somehow got so damned lucky to be with this incredible, amazing girl.

And I know that with every bit of my soul, I will do my best to keep this girl safe and happy.

Forever.

WANT MORE? READ AN EXCERPT FROM HOW TO LOVE A COWBOY

Pete

I closed the ledger and leaned back into the rich cherry colored leather of the desk chair. I closed my eyes and rubbed my temples, thinking about how much easier things had been when my father was around running things at Killarny Estate. It wasn't anything I hadn't become accustomed to over the years. Being the oldest of the five Killarny brothers, it was expected from birth that I would be the one to take over the day to day running of the ranch. While all the brothers were equal partners in running the ranch, it was I who was the most responsible. Ask anyone. It was also me that my dad had turned to back when my mother, Emily Killarny, had first been diagnosed with breast cancer.

At my mother's request, I took on the additional tasks that my father had usually taken care of. Most of it was business, the sort of thing that didn't capture my attention quite like the quiet, meditative work with the horses, but I knew what had to be done. Most of all, I hadn't wanted to let my mother down.

Emily Killarny was a force unto herself, but she had a kind and good heart, and above all, she loved her children. I was aware that I had a special place in her heart when she had gone out of her way to be the best kind of grandmother she could be to Emma. I'd been dejected and alone, raising a two year old daughter alone after my ex-wife, Kelly, decided one day that motherhood and married life wasn't for her. My parents had been so kind to us in the days following that abandonment, and I would forever be grateful to both of them. My mother had especially done all that she could to make sure that Emma felt safe and loved after her mother's abrupt departure.

Back then my major responsibilities had been tending to the horses, something I still loved and wished I was able to do more of, but being the oldest, and since my father had relocated to Costa Rica, I knew I had to be the one to step up to the plate. My mother's death three years prior had taken a toll on the family patriarch, and after suffering a severe bout of depression, he finally decided to make some major changes. One of those changes included leaving the states and relocating to a warmer climate, leaving the green Kentucky hills behind him in favor of sun and sand. Some days I couldn't help but feel a little jealous of that, but I knew that my heart would always be right here, wherever Emma was.

I opened my eyes again and looked at my computer screen for a moment before getting up and heading for the door, grabbing my jacket on the way. There was still a chill in the air that early in the Kentucky spring and it was invigorating to step out into the morning air, breathing in the fresh smell of new grass and the less pleasing scent wafting from the nearest barn. The smell of manure might not have appealed to everyone, but for me, it was a reminder of home and childhood.

I breathed in the air and made my way over to the stables where my brother Alex was brushing out the coat of a two year old mare.

"She looks beautiful," I said as I came up to stand on the other side of the stall door.

Alex nodded. "Siobhan is quite a looker." He brushed her

russet coat to a glistening sheen that caught the early morning sun and made the horse look like a copper penny.

"You think we'll run her next year?" I asked him as I looked over the horse from nose to tail. She was beautiful, but I wasn't sure if she was one of the horses that we would end up taking to the many derbies we were involved in.

Alex shrugged. "Not sure. She hasn't been run that much, and I really think that if we had planned on doing that with her, she should have seen a little more practice at this point in her life. I think she is a great horse, but I'm not sure the derby life is the one for her. However, I do think she is going to give us a lot of talented foals."

Alex was probably the quietest of all the brothers, so hearing him talk this much was a little unusual. The only time Alex had much to say was when he was talking about a horse. Not much for words and usually keeping to himself, he was definitely the most horse whisperer like among us and was more involved with the training of individuals here at the ranch. He was so in tune with the horses that it helped to have his expertise around to help people become accustomed to green horses. While most of our horses were bred here on the ranch, we did keep a group of wild ponies from the Dakotas on one of the spreads of land that was fenced off from the rest. Alex's house was out there and visiting that part of the ranch felt like entering a wilderness. I could see why my parents had given him that parcel when they were divvying up the land to us. It fit my younger brother's personality perfectly, and he was never happier than he was when he was among the wild horses.

"Her mother is Spring, right?" I asked.

"Yeah, and her father was David's Lariat."

David's Lariat had been one of Alex's favorites. A horse that my father had acquired from a Colorado ranch when we were still very young, the horse had been a monster of an animal when we got him. He stood taller than any of our other horses but managed to be faster than almost any horse half his weight.

He was a marvel and had produced many of our fastest horses. David's Lariat had died just a year before, but we still had a few of his offspring around the ranch and would likely see his influence in our derby horses for decades to come.

"Well, even if she isn't going to run for us, she's a beautiful girl, and I'm sure she'll give us a few great runners."

"What are you up to?" Alex asked as he put away the brush and stepped out of the stall to join me where I stood.

I shrugged. "Just needed to get out of the office for a little while."

"Already?" He looked at his watch. "It's early in the day. Why don't you hire someone to take care of some of the stuff you don't enjoy? That's what bookkeepers are for, after all. It would give you a break and let you have a chance to get back out here with the horses where you want to be."

Alex was perceptive with more than just the horses.

"Yeah, well, I might do that after the next couple of derbies have passed. I've got too much on my plate right now to hand it over to someone totally new."

My brother sighed and shrugged. "Whatever you say. Just don't be afraid to ask for a little help when you need it."

I gave him a firm pat on the back and continued on down through the stables, past the stalls that housed our many horses. A few of our ranch hands were leading some of the horses out to graze in the pasture, while some of them were headed to the arena and our track for training. As I exited the other end of the massive stable, I saw Emma atop her horse, Saoirse.

"How'dya do, Miss Emma Lou?"

Emma frowned at me, and I could see her brow furrowing under her helmet. I knew she hated it when I referred to her middle name, Louise, but told myself that someday she would come to think of it as endearing, so I kept up the practice.

She tossed her head back. "Saoirse and I just went out for our morning run. I was about to take her back to the stable and then head in for my lessons. Is Hetty here yet?"

I shook my head. "She wasn't there when I left the house, but there's a good chance she's arrived by now. Better hurry on back, you don't want to be late."

My twelve year old daughter beamed at me from where she sat on her horse and headed into the stable before dismounting. I watched her lead her young horse into the stall and couldn't help but notice how much she was starting to look like her mother. It wasn't a bad thing, but I did wonder how Emma would feel as she looked in the mirror and started to notice the resemblance she shared with the woman who left her—and me—behind when Emma was just a toddler.

I walked toward the pasture as I recalled the time directly after Kelly left. It had been a shock to me when it happened, but when I had a little time to think it over, nothing about it was too surprising. We had married straight out of high school, and my parents had been opposed to the match from the start. Kelly's parents were business owners in the nearest town, and ours had been the kind of wedding that made the local papers. Our courtship had been brief — we dated at the end of high school, and because I was an idiot, I had proposed to Kelly not long after graduation. We married and moved into a house here at Killarny Estate and had had a hell of a time for the first couple of years.

Kelly was wild and looking back I could tell she had been just a little too wild for me. It wasn't something I had noticed at the time, and while it was just the two of us, it was easy to forget that we were stepping into a new world that included all sorts of new responsibilities. Back then we would spend our weekends hopping around the bars in town before heading back to the privacy of our house at the ranch and going at it like rabbits. It was no surprise when Kelly got pregnant, and I was overjoyed, but she didn't seem too enthused about it. Slowly she warmed to the idea, and once Emma was born, I could see that she really did love our daughter.

Things were never the same though. Kelly never looked at me the same way, and I tried to encourage her to go see a doctor to see if what she was struggling with was postpartum depression, but she wouldn't listen.

I came home one evening to find all of Kelly's things gone, a note on the kitchen table, and Emma wailing in her playpen. I had picked up my daughter and the note and read the words through tears as Emma sniffled and buried her head against my shoulder. Kelly was gone. She apologized in the letter, said she was heading to California to pursue her dream of being an actress, and that she was going with her friend, Bud.

Bud was the guy she had dated before me in high school, and suddenly it all started to make sense. We never really heard from her after that, aside from a Christmas card or a birthday present for Emma on the years that Kelly remembered, which were few and far between.

As far as I knew, Emma had no real memory of her mother. It made me sad, but I wondered if it was for the best that she didn't know what she was missing out on. If Kelly had hung around much longer, it would have been more difficult than it already was to get Emma used to not having her mother around.

I had been so grateful to my parents for the support they were during that time, especially my mother. She had done all she could to be the maternal figure in my daughter's life, but she never stopped pressing me to go on dates and get out there again, constantly reminding me that I was still young and there was happiness out there for me if I would just go looking for it.

Her last attempt had been just a few years before she passed away when I had first hired Hetty Blackburn, a local teacher, to be Emma's tutor. The ranch was well out of the way, and it was quite a hike to the nearest school, so I had decided to homeschool Emma. It gave her a chance to be around the horses more and to study at her own pace, which was quite a bit faster than the average elementary school student, according to Hetty.

Hetty was pretty and a very sweet woman. Her black hair and blue eyes were a sort of bewitching combination that was hard to ignore, but I couldn't get back into dating; not then and not now, even though it was 10 years since Kelly walked out. Even if I hadn't already been very hesitant to date, Hetty already had one major strike against her—she knew my daughter.

I leaned against the bright white fence and watched as a group of our horses played together in the dewy field that was filled with clover. The place was even more picturesque than usual in this light. Killarny Estate was really something to be proud of, and I was so glad to have the privilege of being a part of a four generation horse ranch, the largest one in Kentucky, and now, for all intents and purposes, running the place.

One rule I had established for myself was that until I knew I could trust a woman, she would never meet my daughter. And since I wasn't in the mood to start dating yet, nothing had ever made it that far. Sure, I had been with women since Kelly—too many to count—but I was there to get what I wanted and get out. I never went out with anyone that I thought was there for more than what I was because I had more heart than that. But I didn't trust anyone to give me any more than what I was looking for at the moment. It was sex, pure and simple—though rarely pure or simple. I was there for a release, to have sex, hear them scream my name, and then leave quietly. The closest I had ever come to bringing a woman home was the Lawrence girl who I made it all the way back to the ranch with, but we never left my truck. We had made it as far as the pecan grove when I pulled over and had her right there in the cab of my pickup. When we were done, I turned around and drove her right back to her house. But that had been the last one, and that had been a long time ago now.

There was no need to complicate my life any more than it already was and I was certainly not going to bring any of these women into the life of my daughter. She had already experienced enough pain from my poor choices, and I wasn't going to do that to her again.

My middle brother, Jake, came riding up on his stallion and brought the horse to a quick halt a few feet away from me.

"Showing off?" I asked as I cocked my eyebrow at him.

He swung down off the saddle and gave the horse a pat. "This bastard is ready to run!"

Clement certainly looked like he was ready for it. His eyes were wild, but it was clear that he was happy after his morning run with Jake.

"Think about how fast he's going to be with one of the jockeys on him!"

I nodded. "We're taking him to the Waters derby, right?"

"Yup, just a couple of weeks away now."

I noted to myself that I needed to check that out on the calendar. There was still a lot left to do in preparation, and we weren't sure how many horses we would be taking. Clement was certainly on the top of the list, but I knew we needed to have a few backups. Killarny Estate had always been top of the pack as far as producing some of the fastest race horses in the country, but ever since my father had packed it up and gone to Costa Rica, it felt like we had lost some of our edge. I had no idea what it was Dad had that we didn't quite have down yet, other than the forty years of experience. What I did know was that it was crucial for us to win this derby. Things were tight, and if we were going to turn them around and maintain things the way they were around here, or if we were ever going to have any hope of making Killarny the very best again, we had to win the Waters derby.

"You coming?" Jake asked me as he brushed his reddish-brown hair back out of his face and wiped his brow with the back of his sleeve.

I looked at him bewildered. "Of course I am."

He shrugged. "Don't act like it's a given. You haven't been there in years."

"Yeah, well...now I don't really have any choice, do I? Dad is still in Costa Rica, and I don't know the next time he's planning on coming back, so I've got to be there to represent the ranch.

And I think Emma would enjoy the trip to Tennessee, so yeah, I'll be there."

"You're not nervous, are you?" Jake winked at me, and I frowned in response.

"Why would I be nervous?"

"Because," he began, pausing to spit on the ground. "Little Sara Waters is going to be there. I wonder if she is going to follow you around like she always used to when we were kids."

I rolled my eyes. "Sara Waters is thirty by now. I am sure she has got better things to do than chase around a nearly middle-aged man with his twelve year old daughter in tow."

"Hey now, don't write yourself off just yet. You're only a year or so older than her, right? I bet she would be champing at the bit to get a piece of a Killarny brother."

I shook my head and started off back toward the stable, Jake following behind me with Clement.

"Then she can have her pick of the other four. Hell, she can have both Stephen and Sam if she wants them." I stopped and looked around. "Speaking of that, where are the twins?"

Jake shrugged as he continued toward the stable. "Who the hell knows. They're out every night of the week. Probably still in bed."

I knew he was kidding about the last thing. If we had been taught anything as kids, it was that getting up early in the morning was the Killarny way.

"Okay, well. I need to go find them. I'll get back to you about the Waters derby. We need to talk about some logistics getting there, but it can wait until later."

As I walked off toward the other barns to locate my two youngest brothers, I couldn't help thinking about what Jake had said regarding Sara Waters. I hadn't seen her since we were practically teenagers. It must have been a decade or so. I wondered what she looked like now and if there was a chance that we'd get some time alone when I was at her father's derby in a few weeks.

GET A FREE BOOK!

Join my mailing list to be the first to know of new releases, free books, special prices and other author giveaways.

http://freehotcontemporary.com

ALSO BY JESSA JAMES

Bad Boy Billionaires

Lip Service

Rock Me

Lumber jacked

Baby Daddy

Billionaire Box Set 1-4

The Virgin Pact

The Teacher and the Virgin

His Virgin Nanny

His Dirty Virgin

Club V

Unravel

Undone

Uncover

Cowboy Romance

How To Love A Cowboy

How To Hold A Cowboy

Beg Me

Valentine Ever After

Covet/Crave

Kiss Me Again

Handy

Bad Behavior

ABOUT THE AUTHOR

Jessa James grew up on the East Coast but always suffered a severe case of wanderlust. She's lived in six states, had a variety of jobs and always comes back to her first true love – writing. Jessa works full time as a writer, eats too much dark chocolate, has an iced-coffee and Cheetos addiction, and can't get enough of sexy alpha males who know exactly what they want – and aren't afraid to say it. Dominant, alpha-male insta-luv is her favorite to read (and write).

Sign up HERE for Jessa's Newsletter:

http://jessajamesauthor.com/mailing-list/

www.ingramcontent.com/pod-product-compliance
Lightning Source LLC
LaVergne TN
LVHW011827060526
838200LV00053B/3928